D1110131

The Silent Angel

Heinrich Böll

The Silent Angel

TRANSLATED BY BREON MITCHELL

St. Martin's Press · New York

From the estate of Heinrich Böll with the permission of Annemarie, René, Vincent, and Viktor Böll and of Heinrich Vormweg.

Originally published as *Der Engel schwieg* by Verlag Kiepenheuer & Witsch in Cologne, Germany.

Design by Sara Stemen

LIBRARY OF CONGRESS
CATALOGING-IN-PUBLICATION DATA

Böll, Heinrich.
    [Engel schwieg. English]
      p. cm.
    ISBN 0-312-11064-2
    I. Title.
    PT2603.0394E5413   1994
    833'.914—dc20   94-2052
                                     CIP

First Edition: June 1994

10 9 8 7 6 5 4 3 2 1

INTRODUCTION

IN JANUARY OF 1950, Heinrich Böll, a promising young German author yet to publish his first novel, was nearly in despair. To his friend Paul Schaaf he confided how close he was to giving up all hope of a literary life:

> If I were to describe to you my situation during the past three months, you would hardly be able to believe it; it's totally impossible for things to go on this way. My wife can't take any more, I can't take any more— things have gone so far that novels and short stories mean nothing to me measured against a single tear

shed by my wife: that's how things are. . . . Up to now, I've been unable to work freelance, nor do I earn enough to buy shoes for my children. I've simply undertaken something impossible, and I have to confess that I've reached a dead end.

Part of the struggle he faced was the pressure to complete his first novel, one he hoped would solidify the readership he had already begun to build with the novella *Der Zug war pünktlich* (The train was on time, 1949) the previous year. At the urging of his publisher Friedrich Middelhauve, and with the support of a small monthly payment, he was hard at work on a novel entitled *Der Engel schwieg* (The silent angel). Unable, however, to support his family on the publisher's stipend alone, he was forced to break off work on that novel repeatedly and write short stories in hopes of generating an adequate income. And as the new year dawned in 1950, it seemed an impossible task.

We know now that Heinrich Böll was already on the path that would lead twenty-two years later to the Nobel Prize and a reputation as the conscience of his nation. Yet there was little in the immediate future to give him cause for cheer. He had already been warned that the German public had scant taste for novels dealing with the harsh realities of war and its aftermath, and even though he was careful to point out to the publishers that his narrative did not describe the war itself, it was still clear that the novel would offer small consolation to readers desiring to turn their gaze from the devastation suffered by their nation:

The narrative begins on the day of the capitulation and fades to the beginning of the war in the second chapter; nothing is told about the war itself, and hardly anything is said about the postwar period, that El Dorado of the black market and corruption: the novel simply portrays the people of the time and their hunger, telling a love story in a clear and austere style corresponding to the laconic nature of the generation which has "come home," a generation that knows there is no home for them on this earth.

This brief description, offered by Böll to the publishers for publicity purposes, was hardly likely to have allayed any fears they may have had. He pressed forward with work on the novel and sent them the completed manuscript in August of 1950. But, perhaps predictably, they were not entirely pleased. Without ever voicing precise objections in writing, they encouraged Böll to revise and expand the novel, which he did over the next few months, but without ever satisfying them. At the same time he had been working on a series of linked short stories under the title *Wo warst du, Adam?* (Where were you, Adam?, 1951), which the publishers began to set for immediate publication. It was clear that his silent angel was not to find a voice any time soon, and Böll requested that the manuscript be returned to him.

In the years to come, Böll was to establish himself as one of the great figures of postwar German literature. Yet *Der Engel schwieg* remained unpublished during his lifetime. To a large extent, this was because he chose to incorporate much of the material in his subsequent work. Thus, readers familiar with *Und sagte kein einziges*

Wort (And never said a word, 1953) will recognize several elements of the plot as well as characters from *Der Engel schwieg*, including narrative passages taken over almost verbatim from the earlier novel. Moreover, he was to use many of the themes, motifs, and figures from this first novel, expanding and developing them in major works such as *Ansichten eines Clowns* (The Clown, 1963). Nevertheless, the publication of *Der Engel schwieg* in Germany in 1992, on the occasion of what would have been his seventy-fifth birthday, was entirely fitting, for *The Silent Angel* is an important work that offers a key to Böll's entire later development. Like Joyce's *Stephen Hero*, Böll's first novel will be read for its scholarly interest, but it will also be read for its poetic power, its keen observation of a war-torn city, and its insight into the human heart.

—*Breon Mitchell*

I

T H E F I R E G L O W in the north of the city was bright
enough for him to make out the letters over the portal:
. . . CENT-HAUS he read, and cautiously made his way up
the stairs; light came from one of the basement windows
to the right of the steps. He hesitated for a moment to
see if he could make out anything behind the dirty
panes, then he continued slowly on toward his own
shadow, which mounted higher along an undamaged
wall above him, spreading and growing, a pale phantom
with dangling arms, inflating, its head already angled into
the void beyond the top of the wall. He turned right,

stepping over shards of glass, and gave a start: his heart began to pound and he felt himself trembling. Someone was standing to the right in a dark recess, someone who wasn't moving. He tried to call out something that sounded like "hello," but his voice was constricted with fear, and he was hampered by the pounding of his heart. The figure in the darkness didn't move; it was holding something in its hands that looked like a stick—he approached hesitantly, and even when he realized it was a statue his heart still kept pounding. He drew nearer and saw in the dim light that it was a stone angel with flowing locks, holding a lily in its hand. He leaned forward until his chin was almost touching the figure's chest and stared into its face for a long time with a strange joy, the first face he'd encountered in that city: the stony visage of an angel, smiling tenderly, painfully. Its face and hair were covered with thick, gray dust, the blind eye sockets too were filled with dark flakes; he blew them away cautiously, almost lovingly, smiling now himself, freeing the entire tender oval from dust, and suddenly he saw that the smile was made of plaster. The grime had conferred upon its lines the nobility of the original from which the reproduction had been cast, but he continued blowing, clearing off the luxurious locks, the chest, the flowing robe, and cleaned off the plaster lily with tiny, cautious puffs. The joy that had filled him at the sight of the smiling stone face died away as the garish colors came into view, the ghastly paint of the piety industry, the golden borders of the robe—and suddenly the face's smile seemed as dead to him as the all-too-flowing hair. He turned away slowly into the hall, looking for the door to the basement. His heart was no longing pounding.

Heavy, sour-smelling air flowed toward him from the

basement, and he slowly descended the slimy steps and felt his way into a yellow darkness. Water was dripping from somewhere above; it mingled with the dust and dirt and made the steps as slippery as the bottom of an aquarium. He went on. Light came from a door at the back, light at last. On the right, in the semidarkness, he read a sign: X-RAY ROOM: PLEASE DO NOT ENTER. He drew nearer to the light; it was soft and yellow, very subdued, and he could tell from the way it flickered that it must be a candle. Nothing could be heard, fallen plaster lay everywhere, chunks of masonry, and the unidentifiable debris that always littered the floor after air raids. Doors had been blown open, and as he walked on he peered into dark rooms where the fleeting glimmer of light revealed chairs and sofas tossed about in confusion, cupboards crushed flat, with their contents hanging out. Everything smelled of cold smoke and wet rubble, and he felt sick.

The door from which the light emerged was wide open. A nun in a dark blue habit stood near a tall candle in an iron holder. She was stirring salad in a large enamel bowl; the green leaves were tinged with white, and he could hear the dressing slapping faintly in the bottom of the bowl. The nun's broad hand stirred the greens gently; now and then small, damp leaves fell from the rim and she would calmly pick them up and toss them back in. Beside the brown table stood a large tin canister from which issued the warm, insipid smell of thin soup, the foul odor of hot water, onions, and some sort of bouillon cube.

He said loudly, "Good evening."

The nun looked around, startled. Her flat, rosy face looked frightened, and she said softly, "My God, a soldier." The milky dressing dripped from her hands and a few tiny leaves of salad clung to her soft arms. . . .

"My God," she said again in shock. "What do you want? What's the matter?"

"I'm looking for someone," he said.

"Here?"

He nodded. His gaze now shifted to the right, into an open cupboard whose door had been ripped off by air pressure; he saw the splintered remains of the plywood door still hanging on the hinges, and the floor was covered with tiny chips of paint. Bread lay in the cupboard. Several loaves. They had been hastily stacked, at least a dozen brownish loaves, wrinkled now. His mouth immediately began to water. He swallowed hard and thought, I'm going to eat bread. Bread, no matter what, I'll have bread. Above the stack, a ragged green curtain appeared to conceal even more loaves.

"Who are you looking for, then?" asked the nun.

He turned to her. "I'm looking for . . . ," he said, but first he had to open the top pocket of his field uniform to pull out the piece of paper. He felt deep in the pocket, took out the scrap, unfolded it, and said, "Gompertz, Frau Gompertz, Elisabeth Gompertz."

"Gompertz?" said the nun, "Gompertz? I don't know. . . ."

He looked straight at her. Her broad, pale, simple face was troubled, the skin trembled as if too loosely stretched upon it, her large watery eyes stared at him in fear. She said, "My God, the Americans are here. Are you running away? They'll catch you. . . ."

He shook his head, stared at the bread again, and asked softly, "Can you find out if she's here?"

"Of course," said the sister. She cast a hasty glance

at the stack of bread, rinsed the salad leaves and flecks of dressing from her hands and began to dry them with a towel.

"Wouldn't you like to . . . perhaps . . . the administration," she stammered nervously. "I don't believe so. There are only twenty-five patients left here, there's no Frau Gompertz, no. I don't believe so."

"But she must have been here."

The nun picked up a watch from the table, a small, round, old-fashioned silver wristwatch without a band. "It's ten o'clock now, I have to serve the food. It's often late," she added in apology. "Can you wait a while? Are you hungry?"

"Yes," he said.

She looked questioningly at the salad bowl, at the stack of bread, and then at him.

"Bread," he said.

"But I don't have anything to put on it," she said.

He laughed.

"Really," she said, offended, "I really don't."

"My God, Sister," he said, "I know, I believe you . . . bread, if you could just give me some bread—" His mouth was quickly filling with lukewarm water again. He swallowed and said again, softly, "Bread."

She went to the shelf, took out a loaf, placed it on the table, and started searching through a drawer for a knife.

"That's all right," he said. "I can break it with my hands. Don't worry about it, thanks." She clamped the salad bowl under one arm, lifted the canister of soup with the other. He stepped out of her way and picked up the bread from the table.

"I'll be right back," she said at the door. "Gompertz, wasn't it? I'll ask."

"Thanks, Sister," he called after her.

Quickly he broke off a large piece of the bread. His chin trembled and he felt the muscles of his mouth and jaws twitch. Then he buried his teeth in the soft, uneven place where the bread had been broken, and bit in. The loaf was old, at least four or five days old, perhaps even older, plain brown bread bearing some bakery's red paper label; but it tasted so sweet. He bit in even more deeply, taking the leathery, brown crust into his mouth as well; then he seized the loaf in his hands and tore off a new piece. While he ate with his right hand he held the loaf fast in his left, as if someone might come and try to take it from him, and he saw his hand lying on the bread, thin and dirty, with a deep scratch that was soiled and scabbed.

He glanced around. The room was small. White enamel cabinets lined the walls, their doors almost all blown open. White linens hung from one of them, and underneath a leather couch in the corner lay medical instruments. A dilapidated black kitchen stove stood by the window, the stovepipe directed out through a broken pane. Kindling lay splintered beside it, and a loosely piled heap of coal. Beside a small wall cabinet filled with various medications hung a large, black crucifix; the box-tree twig behind it had slipped and was dangling between the end of the vertical beam and the wall.

He sat down on a crate and broke off another piece of bread. It still tasted sweet. Whenever he tore off a piece, he always bit first into the soft part, then he felt the pleasant, gentle, dry touch of the bread all around his mouth, while his teeth dug farther in. It was so sweet.

Suddenly he sensed that someone was watching him, and he looked up. In the doorway stood a very tall nun with a narrow, white face; her lips were pale, her large eyes cool and sad.

"Good evening," he said. She simply nodded, came in, and he saw that she had a large, black book under her arm. First she went up to the yellow altar candle standing in the iron holder among test tubes on a white table and trimmed it back with a pair of curved muslin scissors. The flickering flame turned small and bright, and parts of the room fell into darkness. Then she approached him and said very calmly and quietly, "Move over a bit, please."

She sat down beside him on the crate.

He smelled the soapy fragrance of her stiff, blue cloak. She drew a black eyeglass case from her pocket and opened the book.

"Gompertz, wasn't it?" she asked softly.

He nodded and swallowed the last bit of bread.

"She's not here anymore," she said gently. "I know. She was released a few days ago, we had to have the bed. All the gastrointestinal cases had to go home. But I'll see...."

"Did you know her?" he asked calmly.

"Yes," she said. She looked up from the book at him, and her cool, sad eyes seemed very kind. "You're not her husband, are you?"

She turned aside again and began to leaf through the large pages crowded with script. "She had stomach problems, didn't she?"

"I don't know."

"My God, her husband was here just a few days ago. A sergeant—like you." She cast a glance at his epaulets and stopped turning the pages; she had reached the last one in the book. "Did you serve with him?"

"Yes."

"He visited her and sat on her bed. My God," she said, "that seems so long ago, but it can only have been a few days ago. What is today, the date?"

"The eighth," he said, "the eighth of May."

"How long ago it seems!"

Her long, pale finger now slowly traced the final page from the bottom toward the top. "Gompertz," she said, "Elisabeth, released on the sixth. The day before yesterday."

"Can you give me her address, please?"

"Rubensstrasse," she said, "Rubensstrasse eight." She stood up, looked at him, and held the book closed beneath her arm. "What is it, then, what's happened to her husband?"

"He's dead."

"Killed in action?"

"Executed."

"My God." She leaned against the table, glanced at the leftover bread, and said softly, "Be careful, there are patrols all over the city. They're very strict."

"Thanks," he said hoarsely.

She walked slowly to the door, turned a final time, and asked, "Do you come from here, do you know your way around?"

"Yes," he said.

"Good luck," she called back, and before she turned around, she murmured once again, "My God."

"Thanks, Sister," he cried after her, "thanks a lot."

He broke off a new piece of bread and began eating again. But now he ate very slowly, very calmly, and it tasted as sweet as ever. The flame had gnawed a hollow in the candle's rim once more, the wick had grown longer, the glow more yellow, spreading farther. Now steps could be heard in the hall, the soft shuffle of the nun who had departed with the salad bowl, and behind her the impatient steps of a man.

The nun came in with a doctor, placed the empty salad bowl underneath the table, set the canister beside it, and began poking around in the stove.

"The war's over, man!" the doctor cried. "Over and lost. Take off those rags, throw away your toys!"

The doctor was young, around thirty-five. He had a broad, red face, strangely crinkled, like clothes that had been slept in. Hans could smell that the doctor was smoking, and now he saw that he was holding a lit cigarette behind his back in the hollow of his hand.

"How about a cigarette," Hans said.

"Oho," cried the doctor, but he pulled a packet out of the pocket of his smock; Hans saw two and a half loose cigarettes in it. The doctor gave him the half and said, "Watch out they don't catch you, man." Then he held his glowing cigarette against the stub, and Hans saw his thick, yellow fingers, the split nails. "Thanks," he said, "thanks a lot."

The doctor fished out a few pills from a drawer, stuck a knife and scissors in the pocket of his smock, and left the room. Hans followed him. His broad form moved quickly through the dark hall toward the stairs. He called out, "Just a moment, please." The doctor stopped, and for a moment, as he turned around, Hans saw his blunt, flat-nosed profile. Then he was standing beside him saying, "Just one minute."

The doctor was silent.

"I need papers," said Hans.

"Come on, man!" cried the doctor.

"Valid papers," Hans said. "There must be papers here somewhere, preferably a dead man's. See what you can do."

"You're crazy."

"Not at all. I don't want to go to prison. I live here, I have a lot of things to do—to look for. Help me."

Hans fell silent. He could see the doctor's face only faintly, but in the damp, sour darkness he felt the nearness of the other's warm breath, and something rustled in the darkness like softly falling debris.

"Do you have any money?" the doctor finally asked in a low voice.

"Not yet, but soon, once I . . . once I get home."

"These things cost money."

"I know."

The doctor fell silent again, spit out the butt of his cigarette. Hans saw the glowing tip bounce off the wall; a spray of sparks lit up an ugly patch of exposed brick in the wall, then the stub hissed out in a puddle. He felt the strong hand of the doctor clutch his arm firmly, and the other man's voice said hoarsely, "Wait here, I have things to do." He pulled him to the side, yanked open a door, pushed Hans inside, and walked quickly away.

He was in a changing booth: he groped around in the dark for the narrow, wooden bench, sat down, and ran his hand slowly over the faintly aromatic paneling. Nothing seemed to be damaged. It was smooth and pleasant, then all at once he held something very silky between his fingers, a piece of clothing. He stood, reached for the hanger, and took it down. It appeared to be a soft, thin raincoat. He felt large, horn buttons, a loosely hanging belt, its buckle striking against his leg. It smelled feminine, of powder and soap, and a faint hint of lipstick.

He held the coat firmly by the hanger and let it drape down, feeling for the pockets. One was empty—on the left side his hand passed through the lining into air. On the right paper rustled, and as he reached in deeper he found something flat and metallic; he took it out and hung the coat up again in the dark.

It was a cigarette case; he found the catch and opened it. There were still cigarettes inside. He counted them carefully, feeling them with his fingertips. There were five; he took out two, snapped the case shut, and stuck it back in the coat pocket.

Suddenly he was very tired; the half cigarette had made him sleepy. He stuck both cigarettes in his top pocket with the slip of paper, crouched down on the floor, leaned back against the wall, and stretched out his legs as far as he could.

He woke because he was cold. His neck was stiff, and there was a draft along his legs. Cold, icy air was blowing straight up his back to his neck from the crack under the door. He stood up and opened the door: everything was dark—it still smelled sour and damp in the hall, and the stench of cold smoke and damp debris thickened the air. He coughed. He didn't know how late it was; all he remembered was that the doctor had said he would come back. The nuns seemed to have gone. He found the door locked, went back into the changing booth, and put on the woman's coat in the dark. It fit him fine, except that the sleeves were a bit short. He buried his hands in the pockets, found a handkerchief on the right side, and used it to plug the hole in the lining on the left. He pushed the rustling paper farther down. He fastened the wooden belt buckle, closed the door to the booth, and felt his way up the stairs.

Everything was quiet and dark upstairs as well, except for the calm and somewhat paler blue color of the clouds wherever the sky could be seen. The entire left wing of the large building was blocked off by dangling sections of concrete. Through gaps he could see gloomy, devastated rooms, iron beams aslant, and he smelled the damp, repulsive rubble. He turned to the right into an open hall and suddenly heard people breathing: a few doors were open into darkness, the rooms apparently occupied. There was a musty smell of sweat, urine, and warm bedding, and overlying it all the heavy odor of damp debris that seemed to have absorbed the smoke. Now the sound of breathing and softly groaning men could be clearly heard, and in a corner of the room he saw the reddish glow of a cigarette tip.

He rounded a corner to the left and at last saw light. The shimmer of light fell upon a large, yellowish wall, its paper blackened by flames. To the right he saw the ruins of an operating room in shambles: splintered glass cases, instruments scattered about, a padded operating table half covered by rubble, and a large, white, glass lamp sailing back and forth in the dark, undamaged and silently menacing, like some gigantic, disgustingly clean insect. As he drew nearer he peered through a gap into the room. The large lamp hung on a very thin, black cord, swinging from its own weight, and he saw that it was gradually descending, saw that the large, white, disgustingly clean glass shade was swaying more and more deeply, because somewhere on an invisible section of the undamaged ceiling the staples holding up the wiring were coming loose one by one.

The light at the end of the hall came from a large, multipaned window across which a bedsheet filled with holes had been nailed; the flickering candlelight penetrated it only dully, like a weak, golden shimmer, but large, yellow spots of light poured through the holes, projected onto the opposite wall like giant splashes of butter. He peered in through a slit: between four large candles burning in two iron candelabra a stretcher stood like a catafalque. Lying on the stretcher was what seemed to be an old woman. He could only see the back of her head: soft, luxuriant white hair shimmering in the candlelight like a silver cloth. All he could see of the doctor was the red forehead above his mask, and his arms dipping up and down. There was no sound. At the foot of the stretcher stood the nun with the white face who had sat beside him downstairs with the book. She passed instruments, cotton swabs, all with a calm, almost indifferent expression. Her white wimple floated above her like a giant butterfly, and the shadow of the cowl stood out clearly and blackly against the wall, shifting gently, like a huge drawing of a little girl's bow. Another nun, with her back to him, moved the candles about in response to the brief, impatient gestures of the doctor.

The doctor bent low over the body. He almost seemed to be kneeling, only now and then did his skull rise when he asked for an instrument; then his broad chest rose as well. Something seemed to plop into a bucket behind him, and his white rubber gloves were black with blood; he pulled them off, threw them onto a table behind him, jerked his mask down, and shrugged. The nun standing behind him threw a large sheet over the body and pushed the stretcher around. Now Hans could see the face clearly: it was as white as chalk.

HE WALKED BACK slowly; drafts came from every direction. He could still see the cigarette glowing in the dark opening of the sick bay. He stepped into the muggy air, felt his way past the beds, and now he saw that the windows were covered with heavy blankets. The beds were crowded close together, and porcelain chamber pots shimmered in the narrow aisles. The cigarette in the corner was still glowing. Now he could discern contours, he saw a large table in the middle of the room, bare spots on the wall where the plaster had fallen; and now he made out the face in the corner, illuminated by the smoky glow of the cigarette: the narrow face of a young woman in a black-and-yellow-striped kerchief. The face was so pale that it appeared white in the darkness, and glowed softly. He drew near to the bed and said, "Can I have a light?" He saw an arm in a coarse, blue sleeve, a small hand that approached his cigarette, and he drew in on it. She didn't say anything, and now he saw her eyes up close; they seemed dead, dull, not even the glow of the cigarette immediately below was caught in them. He said softly, "Thank you," and turned to go, but suddenly she placed her hand on his forearm, and he felt her touch, hot and dry. "Water," her voice said hoarsely, "give me some water."

"Over there," she said, and the cigarette pointed at a pitcher apparently standing somewhere on the table. It was a brown coffeepot with no top, and he could feel its weight. Her cigarette lay on the floor; he crushed it and asked softly, "A cup or..."

"Here." He took the glass, held it close under the spout and filled it. She grabbed it from his hands; he felt something repellent in the sudden movement and the way she jerked the glass toward her, and he heard in the darkness the hasty, slurping sounds.

"More," she said.

He filled it again. Again she grabbed the glass from his hand, again he heard the slurping, greedy and unrestrained, and he could feel that the pot in his hand was lighter. Then suddenly her head fell to the side, the kerchief slipped, and a thick, black pigtail was visible. He took the glass from the bed and filled it for himself. The water had a repulsive taste: lukewarm, chlorinated. He heard the sick woman whistling softly in her sleep, and slowly walked out again.

In the changing booth below it seemed almost warm. The cigarette created an intense, sweetish dizziness, a slight nausea, and he crouched down again, stubbed his cigarette out on the wall, stretched out his legs, and fell asleep.

Not long after, he was awakened by the doctor's kick on the other side of the door. "Come on, man!" he cried. "It'll be light soon."

He jumped up and opened the door.

"There's no handle on this side anymore," the doctor said. "Come on."

He unlocked the room in which the bread lay, lit the candle, and said again, "Come on."

Hans stepped nearer.

"My God!" the doctor cried out. "You look fancy enough. Where did you get the coat?"

"It was hanging in the booth," Hans said. "I'll bring it back, when . . . it was in the X-ray changing booth." He pulled the crumpled paper out of the pocket. It was a letter; he unfolded it. "Regina Unger," he read aloud. "Märkische Strasse seventeen . . ."

"I see," said the doctor.

"I'll take it back, for sure. . . . It's just that—"

"Keep it, keep it for all I care. . . . Come here."

Hans walked quickly around the table, knocked over the soup canister, set it upright again, and stepped up to a smaller table. Now the doctor took a piece of paper from his pocket, held it under the candle, and said, "I think this is what you're looking for, what you need. Completely genuine." His grinning face was red and tired, his eyes dull, and strange yellow lines of exhaustion bordered his mouth. His blond hair covered the red skull sparsely, like the down of a chick. He said wearily, "Twenty-five years old, totally unfit for service due to serious lung disease. Your name is Erich Keller."

Hans reached for the gray, folded paper, but the broad hand of the doctor covered it, and he grinned at him. Hans said calmly, "I'll bring the money."

"How much?" asked the doctor. His lips twitched the moment he opened his mouth; some reflex seemed at work, a nerve gone bad. His lips trembled.

"How much do you want?"

"Two."

"Two hundred?"

"Hundred," he repeated scornfully. "Cigarettes cost ten now."

"Two thousand, then."

"Yes. When?"

"Tomorrow maybe, maybe the day after, perhaps even today. . . . I don't know . . . as soon as I . . ."

The doctor stood up suddenly and pulled open the window, setting the dirty stovepipe wobbling. Dust trickled down through the bars of the basement window; now the dark gray sky could be seen.

The doctor turned back around, took the papers from the table, and stared at Hans for a long time. His eyes were tired and restless; somewhere deep within there was a touch of sorrow, a shadow of doubt.

"Perhaps," he said, "you misunderstand me. I'm not in the black market business. I don't deal in dead men's papers. But I need them back. Do you understand? They don't belong to me, they belong in the files, and they check on these things. I want to help you, to loan them to you, but I need some form of security."

"I don't have anything."

"Are you deeply attached to the clinkers on your chest?"

"They're not mine."

"And the uniform?"

"It belongs to the same man, a dead man, I have to take it to his wife. Could . . . ?" He hesitated.

"What is it?" asked the doctor.

"Could you just trust me on this? I'll get other papers. In a few days at most . . ."

The doctor stared at him again for a long time, and now, outside, in the stillness of the city that once had held so many churches, they heard a small bell tolling in the distance.

"It's a quarter to six," said the doctor. Then he suddenly thrust the papers into the soldier's hands and said to Hans, "Go on—and don't let me down."

"No, no," said Hans. "Thanks a lot. Good-bye."

II

HE FOUND THE spot where the building had stood
without any difficulty. Perhaps it was the number of
steps he had taken from the intersection, or some aspect
of the series of tree stumps that once had formed a tall
and beautiful avenue—at any rate something caused
him to stop suddenly, look to the left, and there it was.
He recognized the remains of the entrance hall, picked
his way across the ruins toward it: he was home. The
front door had been blown off: part of it still hung on
the hinges, heavy iron and wood fragments. A section of
the staircase leading upward remained as well; laths dan-

gled from the ceiling. He stepped over a pile of masonry and, at the end of the entranceway, scraped clear a marble step at the edge of a large mound of loose rubble. So one step still remained, apparently the first and last. The pile of debris towering over it collapsed at his push. He cleared off the entire step slowly and sat down. It smelled of sand and dry mud. There were no signs of fire anywhere. . . .

It had been a beautiful, stately building. A custodian had even lived on the ground floor. He looked to the right, where the custodian's door had been, and saw a huge pile of masonry, scraps of wallpaper, and crushed sections of furniture. The dust-covered end of a grand piano stuck out at one point; the ceiling of the entrance hall appeared to have given way. He stood up again and scraped away at a certain spot on the mound of debris until he felt the hard, dark brown Linkrusta wallpaper beneath his fingers. He let the dirt stream down from above and glide past him, and freed at last the nameplate, a neat, white enamel nameplate with black letters: SCHNEPPLEHNER—CUSTODIAN. He simply nodded, went back slowly and sat down again, pulled the cigarette case from his pocket, flipped it open, and took out a cigarette. Then it occurred to him that he didn't have a light. He walked slowly back to the entrance and waited. There was no one to be seen outside, it was quiet and cool, somewhere a cock crowed, and in the far distance, where the bridge across the Rhine must be, he heard heavy vehicles rolling along, perhaps tanks. . . .

In the old days this area had been swarming with people at any time of day, late into the night. Now he saw only a rat that emerged from the nearby pile of rubble, crawled slowly and calmly over the mound of debris, and edged its way forward toward the street, sniffing; once it slipped off a marble slab that lay sharply angled across its path, squeaked loudly, scrabbled back up, and crept slowly on. He lost sight of it as it crossed the street at a spot free of debris, and then heard it rummaging about in an overturned streetcar whose metal belly emerged swollen and bursting between two fallen poles. . . .

He had forgotten that he had a cigarette in his mouth, and that he was waiting for someone who could give him a light. . . .

BACK THEN, WHEN the building was still standing, a simple postcard had arrived. It came one morning while he was still sleeping, on the first day of his vacation, and his mother had thought, It's nothing important. The postman had handed her a whole packet: the newspaper, a few ads, a letter, a statement of account for her pension, and she'd signed a receipt for something or other. Anyhow it was hard to see in the semidarkness of the vestibule, and it was dark in the hall as well; only indirect light entered through the large greenish glazing above the hallway door. His mother had leafed through the pile quickly and tossed the postcard on the table in the hall before she went into the kitchen, an ordinary printed postcard that she considered totally unimportant.

He slept late that day. It was the first day of his life, if you could call it a life. Up till then everything had been school—school, poverty, apprenticeship, hardship—and the day before he'd finally passed his apprentice's exam and gone on vacation. . . .

By eight-thirty that morning it was already sultry. It was summer, the height of summer, and his mother had pulled the shutters closed. Now, entering the kitchen with the mail, she turned up the gas to bring the water to boil. The table was already set, everything neat, calm, and peaceful. She sat down on the bench and began leafing through the mail. From the inner courtyard she heard the faint hammering and muted buzz of the carpentry shop set up in the basement annex. From the front of the building came the steady, almost tranquil hum of the traffic in the street.

The ads were from a wineshop that had supplied them with wine from time to time when his father was still alive. She tossed them unread into the big crate under the stove where she kept wastepaper and leftover wood for the winter.

As she looked over her pension statement, she recalled the postcard lying out on the hall table, and for a moment she thought about getting up, bringing it in, and tossing it in the crate—she never had liked pre-printed postcards—but she merely sighed since she was already examining the account, a complicated statement of which she understood only the final figure, a small sum printed in red, and she saw that it had diminished once again. . . .

She stood up to pour the coffee, laid the account summary beside the thick bulk of the newspaper, poured herself a full cup, and opened the letter with her thumbnail. The letter was from her brother Eddy. Eddy wrote that after many long years of probation, far too many, he'd finally been promoted to assistant schoolmaster. In spite of this, his letter was far from cheerful. His promotion had come at the cost of a transfer to a godforsaken "mud hole." He was already sick of it, he was sick of the whole thing, he said, she'd know why. She knew why. To top it all off, the kids had gone through three bouts of illness in a row: croup, chicken pox, and the measles. Elli was totally exhausted, and then there had been the hassle of moving, and the annoyance at being transferred, which hadn't even improved his financial position much, since he was moving from the best school district to the worst. He was sick of the whole thing, she'd know why—and she did know why.

She laid this letter aside as well, hesitated a moment, then threw the pension statement into the crate and put the letter in a drawer. The postcard crossed her mind again for an instant, fleetingly, but then she'd poured herself another cup of coffee, fixed some bread and butter, and opened the newspaper. She only read the headlines. She couldn't get as worked up as most people, talking about war and revenge. For weeks now the only things you read about on the front page were the flare-ups and street fights, and stories of refugees fleeing the conflict in Polish areas to seek asylum in the Reich. . . .

On the second page she saw that the butter ration had been reduced, and that egg rationing would have to continue. She didn't understand any of it, nor did she understand an article she began reading and then quickly skimmed through, which argued that no one should ever sell his freedom for cocoa and coffee. Then she put the paper aside, finished her cup, and got ready to go shopping.

Bright, blinding light came through the shutters; the sun etched a hatched pattern on the wall.

When she saw the small, white postcard lying on the table in the hall, she remembered again that she'd meant to toss it into the crate, but now she was already holding the shopping bag in her hand, the key was already in the lock, and she descended the stairs.

WHEN SHE RETURNED he was still sleeping, and the small, white postcard was still lying there. She put her shopping bag on the table and picked up the small, typed card, and now, in spite of the darkness, she suddenly saw the strange red marks on it, a white card with a red rectangle, and inside the red rectangle, spiderlike, a thick black *R*. A vague feeling of uneasiness swept over her. She let the card fall to the table; there was something strange about it. She didn't know you could register postcards, too; a registered postcard seemed suspicious, it frightened her. She picked up her bag quickly and went into the kitchen. Maybe it's a certificate from the chamber of commerce, she thought, or some professional group like that, saying that he's passed his exam, something important that had to be registered. She felt no curiosity, just uneasiness. She set the bowl down on the table and pushed open the shutter because it had suddenly turned dark outside, and saw the first drops already beginning to fall in the courtyard, plump, round drops, falling slowly and heavily, fat ink blots on the asphalt. The carpenters stood in their blue aprons in the courtyard in front of their shop, quickly draping a canvas over a large window frame. The drops fell faster and more thickly, rattling now. She heard the men laugh before they disappeared behind the dusty panes of their basement workshop. . . .

She removed the cloth from the table, took the kitchen knife from the drawer, pushed the bowl into place, and began to prepare the cauliflower with trembling hands. The large, bold-faced *R* inside the red rectangle produced a fear in her that was gradually turning to nausea; her head started to spin, she had to pull herself together.

Then she started to pray. Whenever she was frightened, she prayed. As she did, a fitful series of random images floated through her mind—her husband, who had been dead for six years, standing at the window, grimacing as the first major deployment passed by below.

She thought too of the birth of her son during the Great War, that tiny, gaunt little boy, who never did get very strong. . . .

Then she heard him go into the bathroom. The helpless stirring in her breast remained, a clump of pain and agitation, fear and suspicion, and a longing to cry that she had to choke back.

WHEN HE EMERGED from the bathroom his mother was already setting the table in the living room. The room was tidy and clean, flowers stood on the table, along with butter, cheese, sausage, and the brown coffeepot, the yellow cozy, and a can of milk, and on his plate he saw a large tin box with cigarettes. He gave his mother a kiss and felt her trembling; he looked at her in shocked surprise as she suddenly burst out crying. Perhaps she was crying for joy. She held his hand tight and said softly, still crying, "You mustn't be angry, I wanted to make it so nice." She pointed at the table, crying harder, then broke out in violent sobs, and he saw her broad, handsome face immersed in tears. He didn't know what to do. He stammered, "My God, Mother, it's nice, it really is.

"It is," he said again. She looked at him, searching his face, and tried to smile.

"Really," he said, before going into the bedroom. He quickly donned a fresh shirt, put on a red tie, and hurried back out. His mother was already sitting there; she'd taken off her apron, brought her cup from the kitchen, and was smiling at him.

He sat down and said, "I slept great."

She thought he really did look better. She took the cozy off the coffeepot and poured him a cup, followed by a thick stream of canned milk. "Didn't you read a little too long?"

"No, not at all," he said with a smile. "I was tired yesterday, too tired." He opened the tin box, lit a cigarette, began to stir his coffee slowly, and looked into his mother's eyes. "Everything's so nice," he said.

Without changing her expression she said, "There's some mail." He saw the corners of her mouth tremble. She bit her lip; she couldn't speak, and a dry, deep sob arose. Suddenly he knew that something had happened, or was about to happen. He knew it. The mail had caused it, it had something to do with the mail. He looked down, stirred his cup, inhaled more deeply on his cigarette, and took a sip from time to time. He had to give her time. She didn't want to cry, but she had something to say, and she had to have time to recover fully from her long, dry sob before she could speak again. It was something to do with the mail. He would never forget that sob for the rest of his life, a sob that contained everything, all the horror not one of them could have known about then. It was a sob that cut like a knife. His mother sobbed, she sobbed just once, a long, drawn-out, deep sob, and still he looked downward, staring at the surface of his coffee cup in which the canned milk had now spread to a smooth and even light brown. He saw the tip of his cigarette, saw the ash tremble, gray and silver, and at last he sensed that he could look up.

"Yes," she said softly, "Uncle Eddy wrote. He's an assistant schoolmaster now, but he's been transferred, too. He says the whole thing makes him sick."

"Yes, of course," he said. "It would make any normal person sick."

She nodded. "And my pension statement," she said. "There's less again." He laid his hand on hers, which seemed small, broad, and worn atop the blossom-white tablecloth. His touch released a new series of deep, piercing sobs. He removed his hand and kept the memory of his mother's hand, warm and rough. He kept his gaze lowered until the series of piercing sobs and repressed tears had passed. He waited. He thought, That's not what it is. Uncle Eddy and her pension wouldn't upset her that much. It's something completely different. And suddenly he knew it had to be something to do with him, and he could feel himself turning pale. Nothing would upset his mother this much unless it concerned him. He simply looked up. His mother pressed her lips together tightly, her eyes were moist, and now she forced out the words, opening her mouth tersely but firmly. She spoke haltingly. "A postcard came for you, it's out there—in the hall. . . ."

He put down his cup at once, got up, and walked into the hall. He could see the card even at a distance; it was white and perfectly ordinary, a regulation-size card, three by five inches. It lay innocently on the table beside the dark vase of spruce sprigs. He rushed over to it and picked it up, read the address, saw the red, white, and black sticker with the red rectangle surrounding the thick black *R*, then turned the card over and looked first for the signature. It was scribbled illegibly above a long line that read: "District Recruitment Commander." The word "Major" was typed beneath it.

Everything was quiet; nothing had changed. A simple postcard had arrived, a perfectly ordinary postcard, and the only handwritten word on it was the illegible scrawl of some major or other. The greenish light from the upper portion of the hall door made everything seem to float as if in an aquarium: the vase was still standing there, his coat hung on the wardrobe, his mother's coat hung there, her hat beside it—her Sunday hat with the dainty, white veil at the top, the hat she wore to church when she knelt beside him, quietly praying, while he slowly turned the pages of the missal. Everything was as it should be. Through the open kitchen door he heard the laughter of the carpenters in the courtyard outside, the sky was clear and bright again, the storm had passed, an ordinary postcard had arrived, hastily signed by some major who might have knelt not far from him in church on Sundays, who slept with his wife, reared his children to be decent Germans, and who signed stacks of postcards during the week. It was all quite harmless. . . .

He didn't know how long he'd stood in the hall with the postcard, but when he returned, his mother was sitting there crying. She held her trembling head propped on one hand, the other hand lay motionless in her lap, as if it didn't even belong to her, flat, worn, and forlorn. . . .

He walked over to her, lifted her head, and tried to

look her in the eyes, but he gave up immediately. His mother's face was distorted, foreign, a face he'd never seen before, a face that frightened him, to which he had no access, could claim none. . . .

He sat down in silence, sipped his coffee, and pulled out a cigarette, but let it drop suddenly and stared straight ahead.

Then a voice came from behind the propped hand. "You should eat something. . . ."

"You mustn't be upset."

He poured coffee, added milk, and dropped in two sugar cubes. Then he lit his cigarette, took the postcard from his pocket, and read in a low voice, "You are to report to the Bismarck barracks in Adenbrück at seven A.M. on July fourth for eight weeks of military training.

"For goodness' sake," he said loudly, "be reasonable, Mother, it's only eight weeks."

She nodded.

"It was bound to happen. I knew I'd be called up for eight weeks of training."

"Yes, I know," she said, "eight weeks."

They both knew they were lying, they were lying without knowing why. They couldn't know, but they lied and they knew it. They knew he wasn't leaving for just eight weeks.

She said again, "You should eat something."

He took a slice of bread, buttered it, added sausage, and started chewing, very slowly and without appetite.

"Give me the card," said his mother.

He gave it to her.

There was a strange look on her face. She was very calm. She examined the card carefully, reading through it quietly.

"What is today?" she asked as she laid the card on the table.

"Thursday," he said.

"No," she said, "the date."

"The third," he said.

Only then did he realize the point of her question. That meant he had to leave that very day, he had to be 180 miles to the north by seven the next morning, in the barracks of a strange city. . . .

He put down the half-finished slice of bread; there was no point in pretending to be hungry. His mother covered her face with her hand again and began crying harder, a strange, soundless weeping. . . .

He went into his room and packed his briefcase. He stuffed a shirt inside, a pair of shorts and socks, writing paper, then he cleared out the drawer and threw everything in it into the stove without looking through it. He tore a sheet from a notebook, folded it, set it on fire, and held it under the pile of paper. At first there was only thick, white smoke; slowly the fire ate its way through until it burst crackling and hissing out the stove top, a slender, strong flame surrounded by black fumes. As he rummaged through all the drawers and compartments again he caught himself thinking, Get going, just get away quick. Away from his mother, from the only human being he could say loved him. . . .

He heard her taking the tray back to the kitchen; he crossed the hall, knocked hurriedly on the frosted glass pane, and called in to her: "I'm going to the train station, I'll be right back."

She didn't answer right away. He waited, and he could feel the small, white postcard in the pocket of his trousers. Then his mother called out, "OK. Come back soon. Good-bye ... "

"Good-bye," he called, then stood quietly for a moment before he walked out. . . .

When he came home it was twelve-thirty, and the meal was ready. His mother carried dishes, cutlery, and plates into the living room. . . .

RECALLING THIS NOW, that first tormented afternoon seemed to him worse than the entire war. He stayed home another six hours. His mother kept trying to force things on him she thought he'd need: soft bath towels in particular, packages of food, cigarettes, soap. And the whole time she was crying. For his part he smoked, arranged his books; the table had to be set again, bread, butter, marmalade had to be carried into the living room, and coffee had to be brewed.

Then, after coffee, when the sun had already passed behind the building and an agreeable twilight reigned in the front of the house, he suddenly went into his room, put his briefcase under his arm, and stepped out into the hall. . . .

"What is it?" asked his mother. "Do you have to ... ?"

"Yes," he said, "I have to go," even though his train didn't leave for another five hours.

He put his case down and embraced his mother with a despairing tenderness. As she placed her arms around him, she felt the postcard in his hip pocket and pulled it out. She was suddenly calm, and her sobs ceased as well. The postcard in her hand looked entirely harmless; the only human thing about it was the major's scrawl, and even this could have been written by a machine, by a major's mechanical pen. . . . The only thing menacing about it was the gleaming rectangular sticker, standing out in bright red with a thick, black *R* inside, a small scrap of paper of the kind pasted on letters daily, whole rolls of them, in every post office. But now beneath the *R* he discovered a number; it was his number, the only thing that distinguished this card from all others, the number 846, and now he knew that everything was in its place, that there was no way out, that in some post office or other this number stood beside a column bearing his name. It was his number and he couldn't flee from it; he had to race toward this bold-faced *R*. He couldn't run away. . . .

He was registration number 846, nothing else, and this small, white postcard, this trivial piece of cardboard of the lowest, cheapest quality, which even when printed cost at most three marks per thousand and was delivered post-free to his house, meant nothing but a major's scribble, a secretary who reached into a card file, and yet another scribble as a postal official entered it in his ledger. . . .

His mother was totally calm when he left. She pushed the postcard back into his pocket, kissed him, and said softly, "God bless you."

H E   W E N T   O U T. His train didn't leave till midnight, and it was barely seven. He knew his mother was watching him, and he turned to wave from time to time as he walked toward the streetcar.

He was at the train station five hours before departure. He strolled from counter to counter a few times, studied the timetables again. Everything was normal. People were returning from or leaving for vacations; most were laughing. They were happy, tanned, gay, and carefree. It was warm and beautiful, vacation weather. . . .

He walked out again, got on a tram that could have taken him home, jumped off on the way, and went back to the station. He checked the train-station clock and discovered that only twenty minutes had passed. He wandered among the crowd again for a while, smoking, then got on another streetcar at random, jumped off again, and rode back to the station, as if he knew that he would be spending eight years in train stations. It drew him like a magnet. . . .

He went into the waiting room, drank a beer, wiped the perspiration from his forehead, and suddenly recalled the girl at the bookshop he'd walked home a few times. He looked up her number in his notebook, rushed to a pay phone, inserted a coin, and dialed, but when a voice answered on the other end, he couldn't utter a word, and hung up. He put in another coin and redialed. Again he heard an unfamiliar voice say hello and a name, and he gathered up all his courage and stammered out, "May I speak to Fräulein Wegmann? This is Herr Schnitzler. . . ."

"One moment, please," said the voice, and through the receiver he heard a baby whimpering, dance music and a man cursing, a door slamming shut. Sweat beaded his forehead. Then he heard her voice. She said, "Yes?" and he stammered, "It's me . . . Hans . . . can I see you again, I have to go away . . . to the army . . . today. . . ."

He could tell she was surprised, and she said, "Yes . . . but when . . . where . . . ?"

"At the train station," he said, "right away . . . at the gate. . . ."

SHE CAME QUICKLY, a delicate, petite blonde with a round, very red mouth and a cute nose. She greeted him with a smile. "Now this is a surprise."

"What would you like, what shall we do?"

"How much time do we have?"

"Till twelve."

"Let's go to a movie," she said.

They went to a cinema near the train station, a small, dirty theater at the back of a courtyard, and when they were sitting together in the dark, he suddenly knew that he had to take her hand and hold it tight for as long as the film lasted. The air was warm, there was a stale odor, and most of the seats were empty. It bothered him somehow that she let him take her hand so matter-of-factly, but he held it firmly, almost desperately, for two hours, and when they came out of the theater, it was dark at last, and raining. . . .

As he turned into the park with her, he put his brief-case under his right arm and drew her to him with his left. Once more she yielded. He felt the warmth of her small, fragrant body, inhaled the smell of her wet hair, and kissed her, on the throat, the cheeks, and he was startled as he brushed her soft mouth with his lips. . . .

She had put her arms tightly and nervously around him; his briefcase slipped from his grasp, and as he kissed her he suddenly realized he was trying to make out the trees and bushes on both sides of the path. He saw the damp, silvery path, gleaming in the rain, the dripping bushes and black tree trunks, and the sky, where thick clouds were racing eastward. . . .

They walked up and down the path a few times. They kissed, and at certain moments, he thought he felt a tenderness toward her, something like pity, perhaps love as well, he didn't know. He delayed their return to the lighted streets until it was so quiet around the train station that he thought it must be time. . . .

He showed his postcard at the barrier, had them punch her platform ticket, and was glad to see the train already standing in the empty hall, steaming and ready. He kissed her again and got on. As he leaned out to wave, he was afraid she would cry, but she smiled at him, waved for a long time, energetically, and he sensed his own relief that she wasn't crying. . . .

HE ARRIVED IN the strange city around six in the morning. Milk wagons stood in front of the doors, and paper bags with breakfast rolls were placed on the steps by scurrying bakery boys—he saw the boys with flour-dusted faces, pale yet cheerful spirits of the early morn. A few men and a soldier staggered out of a bar. He didn't feel like asking anyone the way, and he followed along behind the soldier; he paused as the soldier stopped at a tram stop and stood among the silent workers, who looked him over indifferently. . . .

He felt sick. He'd eaten lukewarm soup and stale bread somewhere that night. He was tired and felt grimy. When the tram came he followed the soldier again and mounted the platform beside him. He saw now that he must be a noncommissioned officer or a sergeant. The soldier's face was red and puffy, expressionless; thick, blond hair stuck out under the stiff cap. Other soldiers got on and saluted him. . . .

The streets grew livelier, cars appeared, bicycles, and the platform filled with pipe-smoking workers who let themselves be rocked along toward some station or other. Schoolchildren crossed the street with heavy knapsacks on their narrow shoulders—and the tram traveled onward, along the streets and avenues, emptying slowly, until in the end only the soldiers remained. . . .

Finally they arrived at the last stop, between fields of cut wheat and a large garden nursery, and everyone got off. He trailed slowly along behind the sergeant as the other soldiers set off more rapidly.

They walked along beside an endless fence that enclosed gray, uniform buildings. He heard whistles and shouts inside and saw faces at many windows—gray, listless faces—and then a gap appeared in the crowded row of boxes, and a red, white, and black barrier rose before the noncom or sergeant. The sentry grinned; then his faced turned serious and derisive, the red, white, and black pole rose for him as well, and he was a soldier. . . .

ALL AT ONCE in the uncanny silence he heard footsteps; he pricked up his ears and took the cigarette from his mouth. It had turned yellow and moist at the end. Now he held it in his hand and followed the footsteps. They were coming from behind him on the right, at times they faded somewhat, then stones rolled and he heard the firm, steady step again. At last the man appeared at the intersection to the right: a worker wearing a cap, with his satchel under his arm—he advanced calmly toward the overturned streetcar. It seemed incredible, almost offensive, that there still should be people here who went to work, promptly and regularly, their satchels under their arms....

He picked his way to the front-area railing and waited. Now the man had seen him; he paused and then advanced slowly. He came toward him a few steps and said softly, " 'Morning..."

" 'Morning," the man said warily. Then he looked at the cigarette and said, "Need a light?"

"Yes," he said....

The man rummaged about slowly in his pockets. He saw the man's gray hair, his bushy eyebrows, nearly white, and the broad, friendly nose; then the lighter snapped before his eyes and a rust-colored flame singed his cigarette darkly alight....

"Thanks," he said, pulled out his cigarette case, opened it, and held it out to the man. The man looked at him in astonishment, hesitating....

"Please," he said, "go on...."

And he observed the two rough fingers of the man as they parted hesitantly and took a cigarette....

The man stuck the cigarette behind his ear, said thanks in a low voice, and left....

Hans stood smoking at the area railing. He was leaning against it, waiting—he didn't know for what. He watched the man for a long time as he walked farther and farther on, sometimes disappearing behind heaps of rubble, then slowly climbing back into sight. At last he disappeared along the distant avenue, where the trees still seemed unscathed. They shimmered greenly; it was May....

III

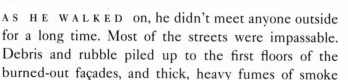

A S H E W A L K E D on, he didn't meet anyone outside for a long time. Most of the streets were impassable. Debris and rubble piled up to the first floors of the burned-out façades, and thick, heavy fumes of smoke were still rising from some of the row houses.

What once had been a ten-minute walk from the ring road to the Rubensstrasse now took him almost an hour. Stovepipes thrust up between ruined walls, wisps of smoke drifted away, and occasionally he met some poorly dressed man, or a woman with her hair tied hastily in a kerchief.

It seemed that not a building had been left standing on Rubensstrasse itself. The indoor pool at the head of the street had collapsed; the gleaming green tiles of the pool could be seen here and there among the wreckage. Here, where the main avenues had formerly converged, he saw more people as well; they were all walking slowly, dirty and ill-tempered. . . .

Behind a row of burned-out façades he heard the roar of heavy vehicles, apparently heading for the Rhine. . . .

He clambered cautiously over the rubble into Rubensstrasse. A baby was crying somewhere behind a window boarded over with thin, dirty planks, and he heard a woman's voice lamenting softly.

The entranceway to number eight was still standing, and a few rooms on the ground floor appeared to have survived. The entrance was wide and deep, the gabled wall had caved in, and the ceiling beams jutted dully into the gray sky. As he was about to enter, an old woman in a green kerchief approached: her face was slack and yellow, and stringy black hair hung down her forehead. She was holding a coal scoop with dog droppings in her hand. She walked on a few steps to the nearest rubble heap, tossed the excrement on top with a tired motion, and returned.

He said, "I'm looking for Gompertz. Am I in the right place?"

She simply nodded.

"Is Frau Gompertz here?" he persisted in the face of her indifference.

Again she nodded, her heavy lids covered her small, inflamed eyes for a moment, and for an instant her face seemed finally dead. . . .

"Follow me," she said quietly.

He followed her into the entrance hall. It was dark, and she paused before him so suddenly that he saw her slack face up close; she smelled of the kitchen, of dishwater, her pupils moved with frightening slowness, as if they were being rolled about with great effort. She stared at him. Her voice was soft and hoarse.

"Just so that you know," she said calmly, "she's ill. . . ."

"I know," he said.

She suddenly dropped her lower lip, turned away again, and went ahead of him. Each time she turned around he saw her thick, yellow lower lip dangling, transforming her face into what seemed a disgusting grin.

They came to a broad, spacious hall, and through a bluish fanlight he saw into the empty, blackened husk of the building. Here below, dust-covered furniture stood everywhere, clothes were scattered across boxes and suitcases and tables, and in one corner an open piano stood like a monster with a thousand false teeth. The woman laid the coal scoop on a table, looked at him again, listened first with her ear to a keyhole, and then called out, "Frau Gompertz?"

"Yes?" A very cold voice answered immediately.

"A gentleman would like to speak with you."

"One moment."

She looked at him again. "She's still in bed," she whispered.

The voice behind the door now called out, "It's all right." The old woman opened the door for him, and he stepped in.

It was a large, high-ceilinged room, and looked very neat and clean. The parquet floor was even polished; the yellow boards were smooth and shining. Above the wide, black bed in the corner he saw a statue of the Virgin Mary standing on a wooden base with a small, reddish light before it. There was nothing else in the room but a chair and a nightstand, and he saw that the damaged ceiling had been nailed over with broad strips of white paper. Dark oil paintings hung on the walls; he sensed that they were valuable originals. He paused at the door. It all seemed too solemn—and too peaceful, too beautiful. . . .

The clear voice said softly, "Come in, please, and sit down."

The woman was wearing a high-buttoned, dark jacket, and her faced appeared paler the closer he came; her hair was very blonde, practically colorless. It seemed thin and disheveled, and reminded him of the wigs on pale dolls. He approached slowly.

She said again, "Please do sit down."

On the marble top of the nightstand stood a small, black crucifix, crudely inserted into a block of wood. . . .

He sat down. He couldn't speak; he opened his coat suddenly and pointed at the field uniform he was wearing beneath it, at the sergeant's braid, the decorations on his chest, and the stars on his shoulders. Everything was still new; the braid still gleamed and the buttons were bright, without a single scratch.

She simply nodded, her face remained calm, embedded dully in the pale hair.

"It's all right," she said, "I knew it, but how . . . you have to tell me how. . . ."

He had already stood up, removed his coat completely, and stripped off the uniform jacket. Now he took the slip of paper from his pocket and handed it to her, together with the jacket. Her expression still didn't change. He looked away from her and gazed at the large window covered with cloth. The sun penetrated the sheet; it stood above the level of the sill, the cloth reddened, appearing to absorb the color red as if it were a thin liquid, gathering imperceptibly, filling every thread of the material, and now he saw that the paintings on the walls were indeed valuable. They seemed painted with light, they showed calm patrician faces above the velvet collars.

He turned back to the woman slowly and was astonished. She was carefully feeling the selvage of the coattail. Smiling, she took a knife from the drawer of the nightstand and began to rip out the seam.

Her hands were as calm as her face. She ripped out a few stitches, then pulled the entire lining away with a long, firm tug; her left hand felt cautiously about in the dark opening and brought out a folded sheet of paper. She handed it to him and said softly, "Read it. . . . "

He unfolded the sheet and read:

Location unknown, May 6, 1945. I the undersigned, Sergeant Willy Gompertz, being of sound mind and body, will my entire goods and property to my wife Elisabeth Gompertz, née Kreutz. Beneath this, clearly legible: *Willy Gompertz, Sergeant,* followed by an illegible signature, a round stamp with the number of a military post and the clearly written words *First Lieutenant. . . .*

He handed the sheet back to her without a word.

"What's the matter?" she asked. "Are you angry?"

He said nothing and looked toward the window again. The glowing liquid had intensified; it seemed richer now, thicker and stronger. . . .

"What's the matter, then?" she asked again. She was totally calm and serious. He looked her in the face. "He robbed me of my death; your husband stole my death. I think I know what the problem is. I couldn't have that quick, clean death; he had to take it for himself, he had to steal it from me. And it was a hero's death, too, a true hero's death, and I had no right to that, I know. I was supposed to live, I even wanted to live—and he wanted to grant me life, but now I understand that someone can grant a person life by stealing his death."

She had leaned back, and her face appeared even paler against the dark tone of the bed.

He went on, "I was supposed to be shot as a deserter. They'd caught me. The Americans weren't far away. Your husband was a military court stenographer, wasn't he?" She nodded.

"Everything was supposed to go rapidly; the Americans were so close we could hear the sounds of infantry fire. That evening your husband came to see me in the barn where I was waiting to be shot. He came with his flashlight, beamed it across the hay, into my face, and said, 'Get up.' I got up. I couldn't see his face, it was completely hidden in the darkness. He asked, 'You don't want to die, do you. . . .' 'No,' I said. . . . 'Get lost,' he said. 'Fine,' I said, and started to go past him. 'Wait a minute,' he said, 'put on my jacket.' I still couldn't see his face. He laid the flashlight in the hay. Its beam struck the dusty roof of the barn; in the reflected illumination I saw his face: it was indifferent. He took off his jacket, took mine from me, and said, 'Go on.' I went.

I hid in the farmhouse across the way, and then I heard the sound of the infantry battle suddenly close by, saw that they were beginning to load their trucks, quickly and hastily, and a voice, the voice of the judge, kept crying out, 'Gompertz, where is Gompertz?' And the voice cried in vain, and shortly before they left, they pulled him out of the barn and shot him. You could barely hear it. Mortar shells were already falling on the village, and tank fire was exploding above the roofs. . . ." He fell silent for a moment. "I was only alone in the village for a few minutes, alone with the dung heap and the dead body, which lay scarcely thirty feet away from me in the twilight by the barn—he'd made a good bargain." He fell silent again, gazed at the dignified, pale faces above the velvet collars, and added softly as he stood up, "You've been making good bargains in this family for hundreds of years, I can see that. . . ."

He stopped.

"My God," the woman said softly, and for the first time she no longer seemed indifferent. "My God, but after all, he asked you if you wanted to live. . . ."

"Oh, yes," he said. "I know, he asked me. They always ask, they're never in the wrong. . . ."

She said quietly, "It can't be helped, now you have to live, and someday you'll be glad you did, God will help you. Thank you for the jacket—did you find the slip of paper right away?"

"I found it while I was looking for cigarettes."

She smiled. "Were there any cigarettes left?"

"Yes," he said, "two . . .," and he suddenly reached into the coat pocket, snapped open the case, took two cigarettes, and tossed them to her on the bed. "There," he said. She looked at him in shock. "Otherwise you'll say I was well paid for the errand that cost me my death."

He turned around and left, and he heard her weeping as she called after him, "But you have to have a jacket—what's your name, for God's sake—what's your name...."

He paused at the door and looked at her again. She really was crying. "For God's sake let me do something for you, what's your name...."

"I don't know," he said quietly. "I really don't know what name I have at the moment, really, I don't know; the last one was Hungretz—what I'm called now I don't know, the papers are somewhere in my pocket.... Good-bye...."

He didn't look back again....

IN THE HALL the old woman confronted him again. She had an apronful of potato peels. "Is he dead?" she asked softly.

He nodded.

"That's what I thought," she said calmly. "Did he finally fall in battle?"

"He was executed...."

"My God," she cried out, "if the old gentleman finds out—by whom, by the Germans?"

"By the Germans...."

"By the Germans, for God's sake." She led the way again, shaking her head, along the hall and through the long, dark entranceway.

"My God," she said again when they were standing outside."Why would the Germans do that, did he say something or other about the conquest?"

"No, it was a mistake, he was executed by mistake."
She walked over to the nearest pile of rubble in silence and threw away the potato peels, and when he turned around again, she was still standing there looking after him.

IV

LATER HE RECALLED that his name was now
Keller, Erich Keller. As he roamed through the city, he
impressed the name on his memory, murmuring it over
and over again, insistently: Erich Keller. When he wasn't
doing that he was thinking how to get hold of two thousand marks to buy the name once and for all, until the
time came when he could use his own again. His name
was really Schnitzler, Hans Schnitzler. The postcard
back then had been addressed to Hans Schnitzler, but
when he was about to be shot his name had been Hungretz; he was to be shot as a noncommissioned officer

by the name of Hungretz. A short time before that he'd called himself Wilke for a few months, Hermann Wilke, corporal. For almost nine months he'd carried a small document factory about with him: an official rubber stamp and a packet of forms that offered everything, all the ration coupons he needed, all the names he wanted to give himself. It was a document factory that would have allowed him to set half a squadron of soldiers off on an illegal march, an imaginary private army, marching toward imaginary objectives, and yet all strictly legal, since the military stamp was real. Prior to being Wilke he had traveled through the region as Waldow, and before that as Schnorr. He chose the names at random while he wrote, as they occurred to him. He created lives that couldn't have been real, and that weren't in fact real, but that were given the appearance of life by means of an ink-stamp on a piece of paper. The imprint of a round rubber stamp on a green-striped sheet of paper lent them legitimacy, and these variants of his self lived on in lists and ledgers without ever having really lived, in temporary barracks and at ration-stamp counters, at soup kitchens and railway-station cinemas. He'd even managed to get socks and a pistol somewhere, using a name he no longer recalled, one of those variants created by an instrument so banal it was barely worth laughing at: a piece of rubber glued on wood, with a few raised digits indicating a number, wreathed about a sovereign eagle that held a tiny swastika in its claw. That was all, the whole splendid affair, and a scrap of paper that put the finishing touch to this con game of the void. . . . He'd had lots of names in the period that had ended just three days ago and seemed so far in the past now; he couldn't remember them all. He was supposed to be shot as

Hungretz, he remembered that as he strolled through the city and repeated his present name: Keller, Erich Keller—an expensive name, two thousand marks. . . .

Later he arrived in a neighborhood where buildings were still standing, buildings with people living in them. Between two damp piles of ashes from which a yellowish fluid flowed onto the cracked asphalt stood a woman with dirty blonde hair and a gray face with dead eyes. "Bread," she called out to him, "bread." Bread, he thought, and stopped; he looked at her. "Bread," she cried again, "bread coupons." He started rummaging in his pockets for money—he found he still had six marks, and he held the dirty banknotes out to her. "Bread," he said. She shook her head. "Twenty marks for two pounds," she said. He tried to work it out in his head while she stared at him, but he couldn't. "Five marks for half a pound," he said. She drew her hand from her coat pocket and began to fumble through a clump of dirty, reddish coupons. He gave her five marks and saw the coupons lying in his hand, tiny scraps of printed paper. "Are they any good?" he asked softly. She raised her eyebrows indignantly and blinked her eyes like a doll. "Of course," she said "don't you know we're at peace now?"

"Peace," he said, "since when?"

"Since this morning," she said. "We've been at peace since this morning . . . the war's over. . . ."

"I know," he said. "It's been over for a long time, but peace?"

"We've capitulated; don't you believe it?"

"No. . . ."

She called to an amputee who was sitting a few steps away on the remnants of a wall, holding an open pack of cigarettes before him. He hobbled over. "He doesn't believe we're at peace," she said. "Where are you from?" He said nothing.

"Yes, it's true, the war's over, really over. Didn't you know?"

"No," said Hans. "Where can I buy bread with these coupons? Are they good?"

"Yes," said the amputee, "they're good. We don't cheat anyone—the baker's just around the corner. Do you want some cigarettes?"

"No, I'm sure they cost too much."

"Six marks. . . ."

He actually did get bread for his coupons, at a bakery around the corner. They weighed it out carefully, five slices, and when the last slice that the woman placed on the scale was too thick, so that the scales showed 270 grams, she cut off a corner and tossed it into a special basket. . . .

And he celebrated the onset of peace seated on a garbage can, carefully and solemnly eating his slices of bread and counting the pennies he'd received in change from the baker. . . .

He hadn't known that bread was so expensive. Slowly, he dug his hand into his coat pocket to pull out the cigarette case, and when he found the crumpled envelope he pulled it out and read it again: Regina Unger, Märkische Strasse 17. . . .

THE RUINS HE had to walk through now were different, hills overgrown with heavy greenery. Small trees grew on them, and thick, variegated weeds, knee-high. They were low, gentle hills, between which the streets seemed like narrow gorges; peaceful, sunken country roads, bordered with crude wooden poles bearing the overhead power lines for the tram and brightly polished rails embedded in the pavement. He walked very slowly down this sunken road, until he met someone who was sitting on a large rock, apparently waiting, beneath a yellowish cardboard sign with a large, green *H* on it.

The man squatting there looked at him wearily and laid his hand in a gesture of instinctive protection on a threadbare sack with potatoes peeping through its holes. "Does the tram stop here?" Hans asked. "Yes," the man said curtly, and turned his back to him. Hans sat down on the curb and saw in the far distance beyond the hills the silhouettes of burned-out buildings and the ugly stumps of churches in ruins. Suddenly his gaze fell on a strange, large metal ring that seemed to have preserved its shape projecting from a hill. The metal was blackened by flames, but within the circle he recognized the undamaged, perverse, stylized bird that had once illuminated the night in the form of a red rooster: the neon sign of a bar with a rooster that seemed to be turning cartwheels inside the ring, a dancing cock whose fire red light always stood out among the yellow, blue, and green advertisements. He glanced back at the man squatting near his potatoes, and asked, "So this is Grosse Strasse?"

"Yes," the man said ill-temperedly, and his broad, morose back didn't stir.

Gradually people gathered at the tram stop. It wasn't clear where they were coming from, they seemed to sprout from the hills, invisibly, inaudibly, seemed resurrected from the empty plain of the void, ghosts whose path and goal could not be ascertained: figures with packages and sacks, cartons and crates, whose only hope appeared to be the yellow cardboard sign with the large, green *H*. They surfaced without a sound and lined up silently in one solid mass that showed its first sign of life only when they heard the screech and ringing bell of the approaching streetcar. . . .

V

THE WOMAN WHO appeared in the door was wearing a long, black robe with an upturned collar, and her pretty head lay nestled between the corners of the collar like a precious fruit in a dark bowl. Her hair was fair, almost white, her face round and pale, and he was immediately struck by her strangely dark, almost triangular eyes. . . .

"What? I beg your pardon?" she asked.

He said softly, "I'm returning your coat, Frau Unger—I've been using it. . . ."

"My coat?" she asked suspiciously. "What coat?"

"It was hanging in the hospital," he said, "downstairs in the X-ray changing booth, it was cold. . . . I . . ."

She'd stepped closer now, and he saw that she was smiling. Now she seemed even paler. "Come in," she said gently, and he stepped into an untidy room with a musty smell and closed the door. . . .

He stood there awkwardly and looked around: there was no one in sight. The bed in the corner behind the door was unmade, and beneath the robe of the woman, who was leaning back against something, he saw the yellow legs of her pajamas. Apparently she'd been in bed when he knocked. . . .

He took off the coat slowly, took the case from the pocket, held both of them out to her, and said in a low voice, "There were still cigarettes in it. I'm sorry. . . . I smoked them. . . ."

She just nodded, and he suddenly noticed that she was neither listening to him nor even registering his presence, although she was staring at him. Behind her thin, bare legs he could now see clearly four unfinished wooden feet, connected by crossbars, the lower part of a cradle or crib. Everything was quiet, and now he looked past her at the window, which was darkened by shutters. . . .

Then the dim electric bulb hanging above her head suddenly went out, and he cried out involuntarily, "My God."

"It doesn't matter," she said. "It'll come back on soon. . . ."

He stood still and heard her pick up a box of matches. The yellow glow of the match illuminated her face. All at once it was darker again; only a steady flame remained on the chest of drawers by the bed. She'd lighted a candle. . . .

"Sit down," she said.

Since he didn't see a chair anywhere, he sat on the bed.

"You'll have to forgive me," he began.

"Hush!" she cried out softly. "You needn't say anything more about it, please!"

He fell silent and thought, I could go now, but I have no desire to leave, and what's more I don't know where I'd go. He looked at the woman. Their eyes rested on one another for a moment and he said, "There's still plenty of light outside, you can save the candle."

She shook her head silently and glanced at the cradle standing in the middle of the room.

"I'm sorry," he said, "I'll speak more softly."

She pressed her lips together and seemed to repress a smile; she said very quietly, "Your voice won't wake it . . . nothing will wake it. . . . It's dead . . . already buried."

The indifference of her voice struck him like a blow. He gave a start. He felt he had to say something, or ask something.

"Stillborn?" he asked, and bit his lip.

"No," she said calmly. She swung back into bed, drew up the covers, and drew the black collar tight around her neck.

"He died," she said, "when the Americans arrived, three days ago. This world's sweet light faded in his eyes the instant a German machine gun shot my window out"—she pointed to the window and he saw the chipped green paint of the shutters behind the jagged edges of the bullet holes; her finger continued on—"the bullets whistled past and hit the stucco ceiling; a fine plaster dust drifted down on us like powdered sugar. . . ."

She suddenly fell silent and turned toward the wall. She lay totally still. He couldn't even hear her breathing, and her shoulders looked stiff and immobile, like wood. "I want to sleep now," she said. "I'm very tired."

"Good-bye," he said.

"Where do you live?"

"I don't know," he said hesitantly, waited a moment, and then continued, "I mean—maybe I could sleep in one of your rooms."

"I only have one room," she said quietly. "There are a couple of old mattresses over there in the corner, and blankets on top of the cupboard."

He was silent. "Did you hear me?" she asked without turning around or moving. . . .

"Yes," he said, "thank you." He found the two old, red mattresses right away—greenish, faintly fragrant straw spilled out of them. He placed them on the floor, stood on his tiptoes to get two rolled-up blankets down from the cupboard. They smelled of the air-raid shelter.

"When you're finished," she called from the bed, "please put out the candle."

"Yes," he said, and when he had blown out the candle he called out softly, "Good night."

"Good night," she said.

Although he was tired, he didn't fall asleep immediately. It did him good to stretch out his legs properly, and to know that he had an ID that would do for the time being. From time to time he listened for her quiet breath in the stillness, and he saw through a triangle between the crooked shutters that the sky outside was slowly darkening. . . .

WHEN HE AWOKE it was not yet completely light outside, and he was cold. The light came through the crookedly hanging shutters, creating a pale triangle of daylight at the top. It flowed weakly through the room. . . .

He was so close to the floor that through the lower part of the cradle he could see her lying in bed, smoking. She blew the smoke in short, light gray puffs into the area of light; it whirled about like a cloud of dust, drifted light gray past the dark objects in the room, a seeming fog. Her left arm hung from the bed with the cigarette, and he saw the brownish sleeve of a cardigan, the small, white hand, and the smoking cylinder of the cigarette. He saw her pale, round face, the fair hair, disheveled about her head, and the eyes, dark and still. . . .

Then she looked at him and said quietly, "Good morning."

"Good morning," he replied hoarsely.

"Are you cold?"

He felt a strange chill run down his spine as he heard the intimate tone in which she suddenly spoke to him. It was unashamed and matter-of-fact, and there was something indescribably moving about it. . . .

"Yes," he said huskily; he realized he could hardly speak. His voice seemed ragged, lost.

She bent forward and threw a rolled-up blanket over to him. It fell beside his mattress and raised so much dust it made him cough.

"Thanks," he said. He unrolled the blanket, pulled it over him, and tucked it in tightly around the mattress.

The light in the triangle at the top of the shutters was brighter now, and the whirling motes of dust stood out more clearly, and seemed denser.

"Do you want a cigarette?" she asked softly.

"Yes," he said, and again the intimacy of her tone struck him like a blow.

She reached under her pillow, took out a crushed pack of cigarettes, lit one, and made ready to throw it—but then she hesitated and said faintly, "I can't—I can't toss it that far. . . ." He drew his blanket aside, pulled up his trousers, which he hadn't removed, and walked over to her barefoot. As he passed through the rays of light he felt a faint, pleasant warmth. He paused, and looked into the empty cradle: the pillows still bore an impression, a small, soft indentation in which the child must have lain. . . .

Suddenly a shadow fell across him and he saw that the woman had risen and was standing at the head of the cradle. She was blocking off the light from the opening in the shutters. It gathered on her narrow back and surrounded her like a halo. Her pale face was filled with shadows. She handed him the cigarette and he put it in his mouth. She was staring down at the cradle, and he saw that her lips were trembling.

"I can't be sad," she whispered. "I can't be sad about it. Isn't it strange"—she looked at him, and now it seemed as if she would cry—"it sounds unnatural, but I don't see anything unnatural about it—do you understand? I almost envy it—this is no world for us, do you understand?"

He nodded. She stepped back and now the light

struck him full in the face, blinding him. The sun seemed to be rising quickly; the broad beam of light was already coming in so straight that the lower portion of the cradle lay in darkness.

"I'm so cold," she said, and he watched her pull aside the covers and crawl back into bed.

"Shall I open the window?" he asked gently. "It's surely bright outside by now."

"No, no," she said hastily, "leave it closed."

He went over to his mattress, pulled on his socks, picked up the coat, which was still lying on the table, threw it around his shoulders, and sat down on her bed.

He took another deep drag on the cigarette, felt the dizziness and nausea well up in him, knocked off the glowing tip, and stuck the rest in his pocket. He wanted to ask her all sorts of things, but he couldn't say a word. He looked past her into the window recess, saw the table standing there, piled high with clothes and belongings, and to the left the cupboard with dirty dishes lying about and a few unpeeled potatoes, and he suddenly realized he was hungry. It hit him like a cramp, a rising hiccup, a gaping, endless yawn from his gut. . . .

"May I have some bread?" he inquired somewhat formally, and then, falling into the intimate manner she had assumed, he asked, "Do you have any bread for me?"

She looked at him, and her gaze struck him once more like a blow. He felt as if he were stumbling backward and being drawn forward at the same time. . . .

"No," she said, her lips barely moving. "I don't have any bread. If there is any bread, someone brings me some later. . . ."

He sat back a bit so that he could lean against the foot of the bed, and suddenly he heard himself saying, "Can I stay with you—I mean for the time being—or longer—for always?"

"Yes," she said at once.

They looked away from each other again, and now she removed her arm from beneath her head, pulled the covers up over her shoulders, and turned to the wall. . . .

"You can stay with me," she said again. "I don't have a husband, and I'm not waiting for one—I've—I've only been with one man—a year ago. The child, it came from him. I don't know who he is, I don't even know his first name, we just said 'you' to each other, that was all. And you, you have a wife, don't you?"

"No, she's dead."

"But you think of her often."

"I think of her often, I think of her very often. It makes me very sad, not because I loved her and miss her now—no, it's not that. It's something totally different." He leaned back, stretched across the bed until he could prop his head against the wall—and he noticed that she drew up her feet to make room for him. She looked at him expectantly, and as he drew the cigarette stub from his pocket, she tossed him the matchbox. "It's something different," he continued. "I'm sad that I never knew her at all, and that she's gone now, before I could say something nice to her. I wasn't nice to her. The wedding ceremony was shabby, everything was so rushed, everyone was shaking for fear the air-raid alarm would sound, and it was cold—the stained glass had been removed from the huge Gothic windows of the church, there was a draft through the damp cardboard filling them, and a brownish, muddy twilight reigned. The Eternal Light at the altar up front was constantly tilting, hissing, and the lamp swayed on the long, iron chain fastened far above in the stone of the vaulted roof. We had to wait almost half an hour for the preacher, and it seemed to me like an eternity of boredom as I stared at the back of my father-in-law's fat, pale neck—a repulsive patch of flesh I was seeing for the first time. Then the preacher came, an ill-tempered fellow who had flung a choir robe over his cassock. . . ."

He fell silent for a moment, put out the cigarette, and the stub disappeared.

"Ten minutes later we were married. Everyone was nervous. At the least sound cutting through the steady howl of the wind, at the rattle or honk of a passing car, or whenever a tram squeaked to a stop at the corner, everyone gave a start and got ready to run."

He looked at her and sighed. "Go on," she said.

"When we got home, a telegram was waiting for me saying I had to return to the Eastern Front. I was barely there for half an hour before I left—even though—even though I could have stayed for a day. . . ."

"You were never with her. . . ."

"Yes, I was," he said. He fell silent again and looked at her; she nodded to him to continue. . . .

"She visited me two months later, while I was lying wounded in the military hospital. . . ."

The memory of that sole night they had spent together was so vivid to him now that he didn't want to talk about it, and he suddenly realized that he never would. He bent forward, propped his arm on the edge

of the bed, turned his back to her, and stared at the wall
on which the triangle of light, now halfway up the door
frame, was sharply etched.

BACK THEN HE had seen the part in her hair below
him, the narrow white street of her part, felt her breasts
on his skin, the warm breath of her mouth on his face,
and his eyes fell forever down the narrow, white street
of the part in her hair.

Somewhere on the carpet lay his sword-belt, with the
raised inscription clearly visible: GOD WITH US. Somewhere lay the shirt of his uniform as well, with its dirty
collarband, and somewhere a clock was ticking. . . .

The windows stood open, and outside on a terrace he
heard the delicate tinkle of fine crystal, heard men
laughing softly, women giggling. The sky was a soft
blue, a splendid summer night.

And he heard her heart beating, close to his chest,
and his gaze fell again and again down the narrow, white
street of her part.

It was dark, but the sky still held its soft, summery
brightness, and he knew there was no way he could be
closer to her than now, and yet he was infinitely far from
her. They didn't say a word to one another; neither of
them mentioned their marriage day, nor the ceremony,
nor the hour of their parting two years earlier, when he
had asked her to come to the railroad station. . . .

He felt that the clock was ticking him away; the ticking of the clock was stronger than the beating of the
heart at his chest, a heart he could no longer identify as
hers or his. The ticking said: you're on leave till the

alarm goes off. It said: sleep with her one more time. That was the point of the ticking clock, and he had even been allowed a bottle of wine.

He saw the bottle quite clearly; it was standing in the dark on the chest of drawers, and it was nothing but a narrow, bright strip of light. That was the bottle, a bright strip of light in the darkness. It was empty, the cork must have been lying there on the floor as well, next to his uniform jacket, his trousers, and his sword-belt. . . .

Later he'd put his arm around her and was smoking with his free hand. She didn't say a word; all of their reunions were marked by silence. He'd always thought that there would be something to say, but she said nothing. . . .

The sky outside grew darker and darker, the soft laughter of the spa guests on the terrace died away, the giggling of the women turned to yawns, and later he heard the waiter clinking the glasses more loudly as he picked up four and five at a time to carry them away. Then the bottles were cleared away as well—the sound was darker, fuller—and finally the tablecloths were removed, the chairs stacked, tables shoved together, and he heard a woman cleaning up, taking her time, doing it thoroughly. The whole of the night seemed to consist of this invisible, painstaking woman sweeping quietly, almost inaudibly, softly and steadily. He heard the swish of the broom, and he saw in his mind the woman go from one end of the terrace to the other. Then came a tired, thick voice asking from the door, "Still not finished?" and the woman answered with equal weariness, "Yes, in a moment . . ."

A short time after that all was quiet outside, the sky

had turned deep blue, and then from a great distance came music.

The clock ticked on. At every minute that passed, he was surprised to find himself still living. The bottle still stood there, an even narrower strip in the darkness.

The woman beside him suddenly gave a frightened start and stared at him. She was very pale, very slender. Her eyes seemed huge in this velvety darkness, and her light brown hair, a child's, made her seem so young. She gazed at him as at a stranger, almost in fright, then she closed her eyes again and took his hand. . . .

So they lay next to one another until it was light. Slowly the bottle of red wine emerged from the darkness, a strip of light that grew broader and brighter until it was fully rounded, and then the field jacket on the floor with the soiled collarband appeared, and the sword-belt with the clearly visible raised inscription: GOD WITH US, neatly stamped around the national insignia with the swastika. . . .

WHILE HE WAS thinking about all that and staring at the wall, the triangle of light mounted a hand's breadth higher, turning yellow, a very intense yellow, and he guessed that it was almost eight o'clock. He turned over suddenly as the mattress springs creaked and saw that she had arisen; holding her pajamas closed, she walked with small, bare feet to the table piled with clothes, grabbed up several things, and laid them across her arm. As she walked toward the door, she paused beside him, pulled on her shoes, and asked him softly, "When did she die?"

"Later, when she was evacuated," he said. He was happy that he could talk again. "The train was strafed, and they found her body on the ballast between the rails, without any sign of a wound. I think she died of fright—she was easily frightened. . . ."

"Do you wish she were still alive?"

He looked at her in astonishment; he'd never thought about it, but he answered at once. "No, I don't. . . . I grant her that. . . ."

She began buttoning the black robe, and threw the clothes over her shoulder. "I'm going to get dressed," she said.

"Oh," he said, and before she went out, he asked, "Do you have another room, then?"

She blushed for a moment only, her pale face flushed strongly red and regained its pallor just as quickly. "Yes," she said, "but I was afraid to be alone last night—the night before last I still had my child."

She went out, and he heard her shuffle across the hall and open a door somewhere. He stood up and walked over to the window. . . .

When he had shoved the latch aside and pushed the shutters open, he immediately shut his eyes. It was bright outside, the sun was strong and warm, and in the wilderness of the park across the narrow street, the luxuriant greenery ran rampant. It seemed to him as if the trees had never been such an intense green, so thickly leaved. The sky was clear and birds were twittering in the bushes; the sound of the chirping, singing birds arose as a loud and confused din. . . .

In the distance, beyond the community gardens, jutting high above the railway embankment, he saw the charred ruins of the city, a dark, ragged silhouette—he felt a deep, piercing pain and pulled the window closed again. Now, within, it was dim and quiet once more, shut off from the chirping of the birds. He now understood why she hadn't wanted to open the window.

VI

HE WAS ALWAYS lying in bed, and he didn't know
what he was thinking about. He was usually tired, but
sometimes he couldn't sleep, and the rain often leaked
through as well; but he didn't get up, he just pulled the
blanket over his head and let it rain—things dried out
again somehow. Sometimes he would smoke too, when
she brought him cigarettes or tobacco, and he ate bread,
drank coffee and soup. They had soup mostly, and there
was often marmalade for the bread. He didn't see her
often. There were days when he didn't see her at all,
then he would just hear her going into the kitchen, and

when he awoke the next morning and got up, he would find something to eat in the kitchen: bread and margarine, and a tin pot of coffee on the hot plate. All he had to do was push in the plug. . . .

But she generally came into his room once a day. He lived in the big room now, and she slept on the couch in the kitchen. She stuck her head into the room. He saw her pale, pretty face, and she asked, "Do you want anything to eat, or a cigarette?" When he said yes—and he always said yes—she would come in, put everything on the table, and leave again. Sometimes he would call out to her, "Wait a minute," and she would pause in the midst of her rapid departure, turn around, her hand on the door latch, and ask, "Yes, what is it . . . ?" He would fall silent for a moment, then stammer out, "I'll be getting up soon, just a few more days, I'll help you. . . ."

"Oh, stop it," she said then, furious, and walked out. And she didn't come in for an entire day, and he had to get up in the morning and go into the kitchen to see if she'd put anything out for him. There was always a note there: *You can take half the bread and half the margarine.* Or she would write: *Soup's all there is, there's a cigarette in the cupboard—*

He was generally hungry, but his hunger wasn't strong enough to drive him out of bed. He only got up to go to the toilet. It was a bother since he had to get dressed and go down the stairs. He was often confronted by people who apparently lived downstairs: a tall, fat blonde who looked at him suspiciously until he said hello, then she said hello as well. Or an older woman who apparently lived in the room directly below his: a tired face framed by stringy hair, who said nothing, even when he said hello. There were apparently men living downstairs as well. He often heard them singing or cursing, and once he met a man who seemed to him of ghostly elegance. He was wearing a blue, well-tailored suit, a white shirt with a green tie, and even a hat, and he said hello, too. Sometimes he would hear cars go by, but that was in the evenings, and he never got up evenings anymore.

Time passed. He felt it; it seemed to him like a fleeting dream, yet one of infinite duration, a strange, gray, insipid drink he swallowed second by second: time. . . .

One evening he asked Regina, "What's today's date?" and she replied quietly from the door, without turning around, "The twenty-fifth."

He was startled; he'd been lying in bed for almost three weeks, three weeks that had seemed endless. He felt as if he'd been lying in bed all his life, in this barely lit room, with its shutters still closed, having bread brought to him, cigarettes, and soup. . . .

Three weeks! It might as well have been three years. He'd lost all sense of time—he seemed to be sinking into this gray, unreal reality.

Then Regina didn't visit him for two days straight; he only heard her going into her own room, and when he got up in the morning and looked for something to eat in the kitchen, he found nothing, not even a note. He searched through all the drawers and cupboards, but there was nothing there. He finally found something she might have forgotten, in an old marmalade jar. It was a strange, dark, lumpy substance that appeared to have once been a powder: it smelled like soup. He dissolved it in water and set the kettle on the hot plate. Even though he was hungry, he felt a faint nausea as the liquid in the kettle heated up and its smell intensified: it seemed to be very old seasoning. It had a disgusting smell, completely artificial, but he gulped it down anyway.

There was no food in the kitchen the next morning either, but a note lay there: *I don't have anything more—maybe this evening.* He waited for her in the kitchen, went back to bed at one point, fell asleep, and was awakened when she returned—it was only noon.

He crossed into the kitchen and found her sitting wearily on a chair, a cigarette in her hand and bread on the table.

She laughed as he suddenly stood before her. "Well, look here," she said, "so hunger's putting some life in you. . . .

"I'm sorry," she said gently then. "Come on, eat something. . . ."

He felt himself blushing, and looked at her sharply. Her pale face was free of mockery; it seemed slightly flushed, and for the first time he wanted to kiss her.

As he sat at the table, drinking coffee and devoting himself fully to the dry bread he was placing carefully in his mouth, she asked, "Don't you really have any papers?"

"Yes, I do," he said, "but they're not genuine. . . ."

"Show them to me."

He pulled the ID from his pocket and handed it to her. She examined it carefully, frowning, and then said, "It looks authentic enough, don't you think you should try to get some coupons with it?"

He shook his head. "No," he said. "The man's dead—that's not my name—if they find out. . . ."

"You have to get a valid ID."

"Sure," he said. "But how? By the way, do you go into the city much?"

"Of course, every day."

"Have you got an envelope?"

"Yes."

"Get one for me, please."

She looked at him in surprise, but rose and pulled a green envelope out of the cupboard drawer.

He stuck the ID in the envelope, sealed it, and wrote on it with a pencil: *Dr. Weiner, St. Vincent's Hospital.*

"This ID's not mine," he said. "Can you take it there for me?"

She took the envelope, read the address, and said, "Yes, but you can't stay without an ID, they'll arrest anyone who doesn't have a valid discharge."

She pocketed the envelope and stood up. "I'll take it there if that's what you want. Isn't it yours?"

"I borrowed it," he said, "and forgot to return it."

She started to leave, but he said, "Wait a minute."

When she turned around in surprise, he said, "Is there some way I can earn a little money?"

She laughed. "You want to earn money?"

"Yes," he said, and he felt himself blushing again. "I have to do something, after all—and I'd like to do something for you, too."

She said nothing, and he saw her lowered lids, delicate black wreaths upon her pale cheeks. She opened her eyes, and he saw that she was serious. She sat down, took cigarettes from her purse, gave him one, and said, "I'm glad you're finally willing to discuss it with me, things can't go on like this much longer. Here," she said, and pulled a camera wrapped in white paper from her shopping bag. "This is the only thing I have left. What's your profession?"

"Bookseller," he said.

She laughed. "I haven't seen any bookstores around, and what's more you can't make a living working. . . ."

"So what's left?"

"The black market," she said, "that's the best thing." She watched his face intently, and it seemed to him that she was smiling, and at the same time she was quite serious, and very beautiful. He felt a painful desire to kiss her. "But the black market's not for you," she said. "Don't try it, there's no point, I can tell that from looking at you. You know?"

He shrugged. "What should I do?"

"Stealing's another possibility," she said. She looked at him searchingly again. "Maybe you could handle that . . . but the most important thing is to have a valid ID so you can go outside, and we can get some ration coupons. . . ."

She seemed to be thinking, then she put the camera back again and said suddenly, "Good-bye. . . ."

He didn't sleep that day. He waited uneasily for her return, sitting in his room all afternoon. He cracked open the shutters and peered out: a spacious, neglected park lay outside, and against the infinite gray surface of the sky he saw a small group of people moving about. A few men and women were cutting down trees; he heard the blows of the ax, and a crash whenever a tree fell.

That evening Regina came straight to his room and laid a piece of white paper on the table for him. He came up to her, put his hand on her shoulder, and stood beside her looking at the closely printed white paper. Her small index finger moved from section to section, and she said softly, "All you have to do is write your name in here, or whatever you want your name to be, your occupation, your date of birth, birthplace, where you were taken prisoner. Everything else is genuine, the right stamps and signatures, and here's the camp you were released from, remember it. But you have to write everything out in both German and English—do you know English?"

"A little," he said. "My God, where did you get this?"

"I traded my camera for it," she said. "It's completely genuine—I got it from an American. . . ."

"My God," he said, but as he squeezed her shoulder more tightly she shook him off. . . .

"And I turned the other one in at the hospital."

"Thank you," he said.

She turned and walked toward the door. . . .

"Regina," he called.

"What?" she said.

"Stay with me," he said, and walked toward her.

She tried to smile, but she couldn't. She stood there quietly as he placed his hands on her shoulders and kissed her.

"No, please," she said softly as he released her. "Let me go—I'm so tired I could die—I can't, and I'm hungry, terribly hungry."

"I think I love you," he said. "Do you love me?"

"I think so," she said wearily. "I really think so, but let me be today, please, let me be alone—"

"Yes," he said, "forgive me."

She simply nodded, and he held the door open for her as she left. He watched her walk wearily into the kitchen, and heard her go straight to bed without turning on the light. . . .

VII

HE COULDN'T SEE how it could have been just three weeks ago: it seemed to him more like a year. The nun apparently no longer recognized him. She herself had changed but little. Her fleshy arm with its childlike hand appeared somewhat thinner and her broad, simple face somewhat sadder, but he recognized her immediately. She was leaning over a large, steaming kettle, ladling out soup. A few young women were standing in line before the steaming opening, and whoever was next would hold the gaping mouth of her tin mug out toward her. The nun herself was enveloped in the soup steam, carefully doling out the hot liquid, which smelled of turnips and a trace of rendered fat. The short column in blue-and-white-striped aprons slowly dwindled, and he could already hear the ladle scraping the bottom of the kettle and see that the cloud of steam was thinning out. It flowed past him through the open door, clinging to his face like fine, hot perspiration, gradually cooling, a gentle spray that smelled of dishwater. The young women departed the little kitchen-house through a gap left by a huge sliding door that was merely leaning against the old door opening. The upper tracks were warped. From time to time a gust of wind came through this gap and blew the steam back, sending it rolling out an open window, and for an instant the nun was clearly visible and in front of her the skinny necks of the two young women who were still waiting—

Behind him a truck drove into the courtyard and a large load of turnips was dumped out onto the ground. The nun quickly left her post, planted herself at the door, and called out angrily, "Go easy there, that ruins a lot of them, people need those.... They're meant to be eaten...."

She was standing right by him. He saw her face trembling with indignation and heard the truckers laughing behind him; he turned around, one of them was shoveling the rest of the turnips from the bed of the truck with a pitchfork, and the driver gave the sister a slip of paper to sign. He was fat, pale, and seemed in a hurry. The nun handed the signed slip back to the driver, stared after him while shaking her head, and looked at Hans. She still had the ladle in her hand; the thin, hot soup dripped from it. "What do you want?" she asked.

"Something to eat. . . ."

"Impossible," she said, walking away. "Everything is carefully rationed, it's impossible. . . ."

But he paused and watched as she served the last two young women.

He was freezing. Snow had fallen the previous day, a wet, nasty May snow. Puddles still stood in the courtyard, and in some corners by the wall, in deeply shaded spots between piles of rubble and the cracked masonry, he could see clumps of dirty snow.

Now the nun signaled to him, motioning awkwardly with the ladle over the opening of the kettle, and he went up to her quickly. . . .

She said in a whisper, "Don't tell anyone I gave you anything—otherwise I'll have half the city lined up here tomorrow," and raising her voice a bit, "come on, then. . . ."

She had scooped half a ladleful from the kettle and poured it out into a tin bowl. "Make it quick," she said, and he saw her run to the door to stand watch. . . .

He drank the soup down quickly. It was hot and thin, but it tasted delicious. Most of all it was hot. He felt tears coming to his eyes; he couldn't hold them back, they simply started flowing, and his hands weren't free to wipe them away. He felt them course coolly along the wrinkles of his face, rolling down to his mouth, where he tasted their salty tang. . . .

He placed the bowl on the rim of the kettle and went to the door. In the nun's face he saw something that wasn't pity. It seemed to be pain, a sort of absentminded sympathy and childlike tenderness. "Are you terribly hungry?" she asked. He nodded. "Really?" He nodded more vigorously and stared eagerly at the handsome curve of her lips in the pale, plump face. "Just a moment. . . ."

She went to a table standing in the kitchen barracks, and for a moment, as he watched her open a drawer, he hoped that she would give him bread, but all he saw her pull out was a slip of paper, which she carefully smoothed flat and handed to him. He read *Good for one loaf of bread, to be picked up at Gompertz, Rubensstrasse 8.*

"Thank you," he said softly, "thank you very much. Is there still time to go today?"

"No," she said. "It's too late. You won't get there before the curfew. Go to the air-raid shelter and wait till tomorrow morning. . . ."

"Yes," he said. . . . "Thank you, thank you very much. . . ."

VIII

A LARGE CARDBOARD sign, lettered in slanted black script, hung on the wall: *Blankets—100-mark security deposit and personal ID*. The air was musty with the sweat and misery of the poor. He let himself be pushed forward slowly in the long line, toward a dark hole in a thick concrete wall with ENTRANCE written above it. The woman at the entrance, who was in charge of a dirty pile of half-ragged blankets, asked for his papers, and he handed her the military discharge Regina had found for him. She entered his name on a list and asked curtly, "Blanket?" When he shook his head, she pushed him on, her gray face twitching in eager nervousness as she snatched the soiled ID from the hand of the next man in line. They shoved from behind, kept coming and coming. . . .

He let himself be carried inside. The interior was already crowded. All the benches and tables were occupied, and he sat down on the floor. He was tired. It was gloomy inside; daylight still penetrated through a crack somewhere, not a bulb was burning. Suddenly everyone began clamoring for light, a greedy chorus of anonymous voices shouting, "Turn on the lights, give us some light!" A surly official appeared in the door and announced dryly that they weren't turning on the lights anymore because the bulbs were stolen every night—he waited for the hoots and howls to die down and then proclaimed house rules of a sort, consisting primarily of warnings about theft, and promised that their trains would be called out in the morning. . . .

He crouched on the concrete floor, in a corner where he was spared the pressure of the flood of new arrivals, and was happy to find a moment's peace, but as darkness fell everything seemed to get worse. Each train that arrived brought new masses of his ragged contemporaries, filthy figures dragging potato sacks and banged-up suitcases, demobilized soldiers twisting their gray caps in their hands or burying their hands in their pockets. Each time the newcomers arrived the door would open and he would see their outlined heads, black and unrecognizable in the dim light coming from the hall. . . .

Later the official arrived again and decreed into the darkness that there was to be no smoking. A multivoiced howl arose in reply, and he cried out angrily, "Smoke till you choke then, for all I care!"

In various corners candle stubs were burning, and the glow of several cigarettes and pipes gave off a soft light. Behind him two women were sitting on a bench, having commandeered a large area about them with their bags and boxes. When he looked at separate individuals, they all seemed as poor, tired, and silent as he was, but as a group they seemed to be loud and obnoxious, and as the candles went out one after the other and only a faint glimmer of light remained from the cigarettes, they all started eating. He heard the women sitting behind him with particular clarity: they chewed unflaggingly. It seemed to him as if they would chew forever, bread at first, a great deal of bread; for a long, long time he heard the dry, rabbity nibbling as they devoured their bread in the dark. Then something both moist and crisp, it sounded like fruit, apples. Finally they drank: he could hear each gulp from their bottles. To his left and right as well, in front and behind, everyone began eating in the dark, as if they'd only been waiting for darkness to get started. It was a hundredfold secretive chewing and gnawing, and here and there a squabble broke out and was quickly quelled. This collective meal settled into his brain like the sound of an accursed condition for which he had no name. Eating no longer seemed a pleasant necessity, but rather a dark law that forced them to swallow, to swallow at any cost, in a hunger that was never satisfied but appeared instead to swell: it seemed to him as if they were panting. They fed for hours, and whenever one section of the air-raid shelter appeared to be quieting down, a new group would be forced in from outside, from the railroad station; it would grow more crowded, and after a certain length of time the rustle of paper would arise again, the creaking of cartons, a hasty rummaging about in sacks and packages, locks snapping open, and the repulsive gurgle of bottles in dark secrecy. . . .

Later they whispered, murmurs in the darkness, recalling memories of happy hoardings, regret for their dwindling provisions. . . .

His forehead was bathed in sweat, although he was freezing. He'd grabbed the corner of a blanket to sit on and was leaning back against a swollen backpack; he felt potatoes, like the bones of a mysterious skeleton. Some people were still smoking; the glowing tips of the cigarettes seemed to increase in number, the air was turning thick and foul. Later the soft drone of a concertina came from a corner. A voice called out loudly, " 'Erika,' play 'Erika' for us. . . ." The man with the concertina played "Erika." Others called out for different songs, and the man asked for payment in a hoarse voice. Then invisible offerings were passed along to him in the darkness, placed in invisible hands and sent off on a brisk and silent journey into the gloom: a slice of bread or an apple, half a gherkin or a cigarette butt. Suddenly a quarrel broke out somewhere, curses and a fistfight over one of the gratuities that hadn't been passed on, at any rate the concertina player denied having received it and was refusing to play the tune. The point where the gift had disappeared was quickly located; the movements of the combatants stood out against the dark mass, a threatening wave of pushing and shoving people. Then things quieted down and the concertinist played for someone else.

The two women behind him appeared to have already fallen asleep. They were completely silent; farther back he heard the lascivious giggle of a pair of lovers, the concertina died away, and the glowing tips of the cigarettes decreased in number. He felt about in the dark at his side and came across a few formless bundles, and it was unclear if they were sacks or human beings....

Later on he must have fallen asleep. He was awakened suddenly by a sharp cry: someone had stepped on someone else. There seemed to be a scuffle, during which a piece of luggage disappeared. A man's high-pitched voice called out excitedly, "My suitcase, my suitcase...I have to catch a train, the two-forty!" Several voices joined in. "The two-forty, we have to go, too." There was a wild shuffle in the darkness and the man's voice kept crying out for his suitcase. Then the door opened, and he saw a number of men standing in the hall, illuminated by the dim bulb, and the man's voice cried out, "Police! Police! My suitcase...."

It grew quiet as a mouse as two police helmets forced their way forward through the crowd, then the sharp, bright beam of a large flashlight flitted through the room, illuminating motes of dust and the cowering, expectant throng, who suddenly appeared quite humble, as if in prayer, their faces turned toward the light.

The policeman's voice spoke calmly and clearly. "All right, if that suitcase isn't..." But by then the man seemed already to have the case back in hand. He called out, "Here it is, I've got it," and voices yelled out at him from the crowd, "You old fool, pay attention next time, you stupid idiot...."

The door was closed and all was dark again, but from that point on he couldn't sleep. Every fifteen minutes there was some commotion or other, restlessness spread like a wave, trains were announced, people called out for friends, shouted their way through to their bags, and the air in the concrete block seemed to keep growing thicker and nastier. . . .

From time to time he wiped the sweat from his brow, while realizing that the lower half of his body was cold. Both the blanket and the backpack he'd been leaning against were gone. He slid farther along until he ran into something; he bent over it to see if it was living or dead, and smelled the sharp, pungent odor of onions. He could feel that it was a large basket, sewn shut. He sat on the basket—just to sit down was wonderful. He drew up his legs, let his head fall to his chest, and fell asleep again for a short time, until someone simply shoved him off the basket. "Nervy bastard," said a voice, and he caught himself as he tumbled to the stony floor. Then he crawled aside, curled up, and waited for a while. . . .

The open spaces were greater now, and he crawled on until he heard a person breathing. He felt his way slowly forward, touched the calf of a leg, a shoe: it was a woman's shoe, a high heel and a small foot, and he leaned forward where her face must be. Her warm breath met him, he held his hands in the realm of that warm breath, bent lower, but could see nothing, then he recognized in the scent of this unknown woman, without knowing her age or appearance, a soapy smell, a faint fragrance of perfume and soap. He remained bowed over her, and he held his face close to her breath. The breath was warm, calm, and the pleasant fragrance of soap seemed to grow stronger and stronger. He turned sideways to her and pressed his face into her coat: musk, a touch of peppermint—the strong and pleasant scent put him to sleep. . . .

When he awoke again the room was being cleared; the unknown woman beside him was gone, and he let himself be carried out by the crowd. Once more he had to stop at the table where the dirty blankets were piled, had to show his papers and wait while they checked to see if he had been given a blanket; a man now stood at the table, an old, surly invalid with a cold pipe clamped in his teeth, dully gathering in the blankets and counting money into filthy, outstretched hands. . . .

It was very bright outside, warmer, and when he started to look for the slip of paper, he immediately broke out in a cold sweat. He couldn't find it; he searched hastily, feverishly, and felt how strong and mortal his fear was, the fear of bread lost or stolen. His heart raced, and he almost broke into tears when he finally discovered the tiny, folded slip in his upper breast pocket. He unfolded it, smoothed it out carefully, and kept walking: *Good for one loaf of bread, to be picked up at* . . . His heart was still pounding as he walked on. . . .

IX

HIS HEART KEPT on pounding. He was still thinking about the bread, and his heartbeat was like the gently painful yet pleasant throbbing of a wound: a large, raw spot in his chest, his heart. He walked as quickly as he could, choosing the streets with narrow passages cleared through them, and by nine o'clock he was already at the street that led to Rubensstrasse. He had to smile as he thought of the woman. What would she say when he showed up and handed her the voucher for the bread? She would recognize him, of course. He knew that. Maybe she would offer him money, a lot of money. Money enough for him to buy a proper, valid ID, one with his real name, a piece of paper that was authentic, insofar as a purchased piece of paper could be authentic. But what set his heart pounding even more than the thought of the ID he could buy was the thought of bread: real bread. As long as he only had the voucher, it wasn't bread. He wanted to feel it, to eat it, to break off a piece of it, to take it to Regina. Bread, soft and sweet smelling, even the brown crust of the baked dough, and sweet tasting, sweet as only bread could be. With a strange joy that had almost passed beyond the physical, he thought of the bread that he had eaten at the nun's two weeks ago. Yesterday he'd gone out to scare up something to eat. He'd promised Regina he would, but he knew he wouldn't be able to find much. He had no money and nothing to trade with, but even so he would be bringing her a loaf of bread, perhaps several loaves of bread. Perhaps she would give him money, a lot of money, and he would be able to buy a lot of bread with it. The price of bread had risen rapidly since the war had ended. Peace was driving the prices up. But even so, bread was available, it was just expensive.

He'd already decided not to buy an ID, just bread. After all, he had an ID for now, a fine scrap of paper, a document Regina had traded her camera for. Too bad, he thought, it might have been better to buy bread. . . .

He sat down on the rubble of the indoor pool to let the beating of his heart return to normal; this raw circle in his chest seemed to him like an expanding, deepening wound, its pain a strange sweetness. . . .

The green tiles of the public pool had been washed clean by the rain and snow of the last few days. They gleamed in the sunshine. The door to a changing room was lying there, painted green, bright green with a black-and-white enameled plate bearing a number.

The date of the destruction of any particular ruin could be determined by its overgrowth: it was a question of botany. This heap of rubble was naked and barren, raw stone, newly broken masonry, piled thickly, violently, with iron beams jutting out, showing scarcely a spot of rust. There wasn't a blade of grass to be seen; while in other places trees were already growing, charming little trees in bedrooms and kitchens, close by the rusty shell of the burned-out stove. Here there was only naked destruction, desolate and terribly empty, as if the breath of the bomb still hung in the air. Only the tiles, those that had survived, gleamed in innocence.

He caught himself beginning to speculate about how much money the woman might give him: a thousand, he thought at first, then it was several thousand, and he was annoyed that he hadn't accepted her offer to help back then. She obviously had a great deal of money. Her husband's will must be worth a few hundred thousand marks to her, and he, he'd paid for it with his death, he'd paid plenty for it. Back then, fourteen days ago; it seemed so far in the past now, there'd still been a war on then, one still in progress, and the certainty that the war was over made those fourteen days seem old and long. He peered into this brief past as at a picture held before him, infinitely reduced in size. It seemed more distant than Greek history, which had always struck him as so far back in time.

Two youths had now climbed over the rubble and were starting to take apart the cubicle door that had been blown off. They went to work skillfully, using a hammer to knock the frame loose from the glue, pulling the panels out of the grooves, and arranging the door into a small, flat packet of wood.

He stood up to pick his way back into the street. Bread, he thought, I'm going to eat bread for sure—and I'll get some money; now he was actually counting on the money, a decent amount of it, an installment payment on his death, one that would surely be worth at least twenty loaves. . . .

As he entered the vestibule of the building he could feel that his hands, clutching the voucher, were damp with perspiration: the typing was slightly smudged as he now smoothed the piece of paper and knocked at the door.

For a long time he heard nothing—much too long it seemed to him—and he knocked again more loudly. The blows disappeared without an echo into the overcrowded hall; again he heard nothing, and he struck the door three times loudly with the heel of his shoe. He heard the panel vibrate faintly at the top of the doorframe and there was the sound of plaster trickling down. . . .

Then finally a noise came from the door to the left, the one that led into the woman's room, and he was shocked to hear the hard, firm tread of a man. The door opened, a face appeared, the broad, pale face of a man with his mouth opened nervously. . . .

That was a thing that had often bothered him, and that he found hard to bear: he couldn't forget a face. They all trailed after him, and he recognized them the instant they reappeared. Somewhere in his unconscious they glided along, especially those he saw only once in passing. They swam about like indistinct, gray fish among the algae of a murky pool. Sometimes their silent heads would shove up close to the surface—but they would finally emerge, standing before him clearly and ineluctably, when he actually saw them again. It was as if their mirror image first raised itself clearly and sharply when they themselves appeared within the painfully crowded sector his eye commanded. They all returned: the face of a streetcar conductor who once sold him a ticket years ago turned into the face of a private lying beside him in sick bay. The lice had crawled out of bandages around the fellow's head back then, wallowing equally in fresh and clotted blood, lice that crawled peacefully along his neck, across his unconscious face. He saw them clambering over his ear, bold, reckless creatures that slipped and fell, caught themselves again on his shoulder; on the ear of the same man who seven years earlier, three thousand kilometers to the west, had sold him a transfer: a narrow, suffering face, that back then had been ruddy and optimistic. . . .

But the broad, pale face of this man with his mouth opened nervously hadn't changed. Neither war nor destruction had managed to scathe it: the doughy surface of academic calm, eyes that knew they knew something, and as a single point of faint pain the slightly opened, finely curved lips, whose pain might well have been disgust, a particularly pleasurable disgust. In the pallid light of the darkened hall the face seemed to him truly like the head of a large, pale carp, rising up in the pond, silent and sure, while his hands remained below in the thick darkness of the room. This was Herr Doktor Professor Fischer, a customer in the bookshop where he had learned his trade, and whom he had been allowed to wait on only once, as an advanced apprentice, for Fischer knew a thing or two about books. He was a philologist, a lawyer, the editor of a journal, had a deep and not totally unproductive inclination toward the study of Goethe, and was held in those days to be the unofficial adviser of His Eminence the cardinal in cultural matters. This face he had seen just once at close range, otherwise only fleetingly, passing by in the shop before disappearing into the boss's private office. That was almost eight years ago, but he recognized it immediately; the line had jerked up like lightning and fished out this head.

"What do you want?" asked the face. . . .

"Bread," he said, and handed him the voucher as if he were at a counter.

"There's no more bread."

He didn't understand. "Bread," he said, "but the nun—I'm supposed to—"

"No," said the voice with calm matter-of-factness. "No, there's no more bread."

Now the hands emerged from the lower depths; long hands with slender fingers, they surfaced and held the voucher that represented a loaf of bread, and the fingers tore up the voucher, not simply tearing it once with a sharp, short rip, but tearing it crosswise, four and five times, repeatedly, with pleasure—you could tell that. It fell to the floor like confetti, whitish, scattering like bread crumbs. . . .

"There's your bread," said the voice.

It didn't sink in until the door slammed shut, a huge, wobbly piece of wood, glued together with framing sections, pieces of pasteboard, and glass, which now rattled and rocked, bringing down a new trickle of invisible plaster. . . .

He stood there for a long time, trying to feel something: hate or rage or pain, but he felt nothing. Perhaps I'm dead, he thought. But he wasn't dead—he came to himself fully when he kicked the door and felt the pain of the blow in his toe. But he could discover no hate, not even rage, only pain. . . .

X

AS FISCHER STEPPED back into the room, Elisabeth turned her face from the wall and asked softly, "Who was it?"

"A beggar," he said, and sat down again.

"Did you give him anything?"

"No," he said.

She sighed and turned her face back to the wall. The curtains had been pulled open, and in the large, black window frames stood the fantasylike image of the ruins: smoke-blackened flanks of buildings, cracked gables that seemed about to fall—overgrown mounds that had been ripped apart a second time, leaving only a few spots where the green was mossy and peaceful. . . .

"You didn't give him anything—who was it?"

"I don't know," he said. "Just some man. . . ."

She began crying softly, and he pricked up his ears. She hadn't cried up till then: he saw her slender neck with her uncombed hair, the trembling shoulders, and heard the strange, ragged sound of her sobs. He was astonished, and somehow he felt it disgusting that she allowed herself to be so carried away by sentimentality.

"You mustn't be angry," he said, "but I want to reach some kind of a resolution, you see, whatever it is. Personally I really don't care what you do, although I think money's too serious a matter to get sentimental over. As I've said: our mutual father-in-law will be satisfied if you give oral assurance that you consider Willy temporarily intestate and give up control of his money and goods. Just orally, you understand, you can't ask for a more obliging attitude than that—otherwise"—he broke off because she suddenly turned her face to him again and he was surprised by her determined look—"the result would be a legal duel, and"—he laughed—"I don't think it very probable that you would win, given the present evidence. . . ."

"I could try to find the man who brought me Willy's testament." She blushed at the memory of the scene she had made with him.

"Of course," he said, "but you're unlikely to find him, and after all, what do you expect to learn from him?"

"The place where Willy was executed. He's probably buried there as well. Someone must have buried him."

"Not bad," he said, "not bad at all." He fell silent for a moment, thinking, and then asked, "Well, tell me then: will you let this nonsense about giving the money away rest for the moment, content yourself with two thousand marks a month, and—"

"You mean a kind of cease-fire—it's all right by me; by the way," she said softly, "if I could do what I wanted right now, I'd slap you right in the face. . . . "

"That wouldn't be very Christian. . . ."

"I know," she said, and felt her tears suddenly dried by an inner fire. "Or rather, I'm not sure I do know. I think plenty of good Christians have hit plenty of people like you in the face, and that it wasn't unchristian of them—but there's just one problem: I'm not a good Christian and they were. . . ."

"That's right," he said. "What you have are humane impulses, and humane impulses are no substitute for the spontaneous passions of religion. . . ."

"Oh, yes," she said, and gave him a strange, almost contemptuous look. "You can explain everything, your type can always explain everything, but I hope a time will come when you'll have a thing or two explained to you. . . ."

"Well put, but I hope I also have a reasonable prospect to be considered a good Christian, there are, thank God, other authorities than you in the matter." He laughed quietly.

She turned back to the wall. I *am* going to slap him in the face, she thought. . . .

"By the way," he said, searching in his pocket for a cigar, "just why do you want to hit me so badly?"

She said nothing; he fiddled at lighting his cigar and looked for someplace where he could tap his fingers, but the nightstand was too small, the space on it was taken up by the crucifix, a glass of water, and a plate with bread crumbs. He tapped on the arm of the chair, but the surface was too small. His fingers kept slipping off and he felt himself blushing; it made him nervous if he didn't have a place to tap his fingers. . . .

"Why?" he asked.

"Because you didn't give anything to that beggar, but let's just drop it," she said wearily. "I've agreed to a cease-fire with you. . . ."

"You wouldn't let us have the will for a while by any chance, would you?" he said softly. "I mean. . . ."

She turned around quickly, forcefully, and he was shocked to see her laughing. "No," she said, "since it's such a worthless document, it wouldn't be of any use to you. . . ."

"Well, we could have it examined; it was witnessed, after all. . . ."

"Yes," she said.

"You can go," she said. "I'm very tired. I'm as sick as ever, and I didn't get any sleep last night."

He stuck his cigar in his mouth and pulled on his coat.

"By the way, how's my goddaughter Elisabeth?" she asked.

The tone of her voice caused him to pause in the midst of his motion, with his coat halfway over his shoulder; he took the cigar from his mouth, laid it on the edge of the nightstand, and stepped closer to the bed.

"How do you happen to know," he asked as calmly as possible, "that's she's sick?"

"Is she sick?"

"Yes."

"What's wrong with her?"

"She had a bad accident on her bicycle—with severe internal hemorrhaging. . . ."

"Severe internal hemorrhaging? That's very bad in her condition."

"In her condition?" he asked in a low voice. "What's that supposed to mean?"

He seldom lost his self-control, almost never when he was talking to a woman, but now he felt his face twitch; his hands had gone limp and were damp with perspiration.

"I mean that she's expecting, was expecting," she said calmly.

He pulled his coat on hastily, took his cigar from the edge of the nightstand, and said, "I really do think you're crazy, really . . . do you think . . . ?"

He made an impatient gesture, because she'd started crying again; he detested the open expression of inner emotion.

"Of course I think so," she said softly. "I'd believe anything of a man who would turn a beggar away from the door. . . . Now leave."

He walked out rapidly.

XI

SHE GAVE THE porter the card and watched as the suspicious face bent over it: the big, reddish nose seemed clamped to the forehead, and the forehead lost itself in a yellowish, bald pate. Then the face lifted again and stood sharp and round before her.

"Room fifteen, OP," said the voice, "around to the right."

She went around to the right past the locked sickrooms, turned to the left, and stopped before a narrow door with *OP* written in red pencil on the cracked varnish. She knocked and a voice cried out, "Come in."

Inside all was quiet. A nun was bending over a steaming sterilization case, fishing out instruments with a pair of tongs. The doctor was sitting wearily on a chair, smoking. She inhaled the strong odor of the tobacco greedily, and for the first time she felt hunger, a strange mixture of nausea and fatigue that rose in her like a feeble yawn, and she didn't hear the doctor's question.

"What is it you want?" he asked curtly for a second time, when she had closed her mouth again with an effort.

She stepped nearer and gave him the card.

"Oh, yes," he said, "I beg your pardon. Fräulein Unger?"

"Yes," she said.

He took the cigarette from his mouth, walked over to his desk, and took out a brown index card from a wooden box.

"Yes," he said, "Unger. Your blood sample was excellent. The analysis showed nothing negative. I made an appointment for you today because we—You still want to give blood, even now?"

"Of course," she said.

"Well, two weeks have passed." He shrugged his shoulders and sighed. "A few things have changed in the meantime that might cause a person to retract the offer. So you're still willing?"

"Yes," she said.

"Good, you can disrobe. Upper body."

She shed her coat, unbuttoned her blouse, and laid them both on the mobile operating table standing beside her.

"All right," cried the doctor, "that's fine." She felt his strong hand testing her muscles, taking her pulse, and flinched slightly as the cold stethoscope touched her chest.

"By the way, Fräulein Unger," said the doctor, with a tired and pensive look, "didn't you leave your coat hanging here?"

"Yes."

"Did you get it back?"

"Yes."

"An honest man."

"Yes, an honest man."

He removed the stethoscope, nodded to her, and said, "No problems. Your general state of health is acceptable. You can put your clothes back on; what type was it again?"

"O."

"Excellent, I can use you yet this morning. Is that all right? For Fischer," he called out to the nun, "what do you think?"

As she pulled her blouse back on, she saw the nun's white wimple nod.

The doctor looked at her in his tired, kindly manner. "You're in luck. Herr Fischer has promised a special bonus to the person who gives blood for his daughter, beyond the usual payment of course. How much was it, Sister?"

"Fifteen hundred marks," said the sister. She laid the heavy nickel-plated cover over the instrument case and turned around. "Fifteen hundred marks," she said again. "Herr Fischer is a rich man."

"A fisher for money," the doctor said, stubbing out his cigarette with a laugh, "not a fisher of men."

The nun shook her head and looked at him in dis-

approval. "You might as well just stay here, the transfusion is scheduled for ten, isn't it?"

"Yes," said the doctor, "I'm ready anytime. Did you
eat breakfast?"

"No," said Regina.

"Could we get this young woman something to eat?"

"No," said the nun, "that's not possible." Her large
cowl shook back and forth energetically.

"Perhaps as a small advance on the payment? It
wouldn't do to have her start feeling faint during the
procedure."

"We really can't," said the sister, "believe me. The
payment is in coupons, it doesn't even come from us, it
comes from the Department of Economic Affairs. All
she gets here is a voucher."

The doctor shrugged. "Then we might be better off
with the young man from Room A. At least he's had
something to eat."

"No, no," Regina called out quickly.

Both of them looked at her in surprise. "What is it?"
asked the doctor.

"I'd very much like to do it—I . . . I won't have any
problem. . . ."

"It's fine with me, what do you think, Sister?"

The sister shrugged her shoulders.

"Let's get started then."

When the sister had left the room, he lit a new cigarette. "I'd gladly offer you one," he said, "but I don't
know, I think. . . ."

"No, thanks, it would make me sick, thank you."

Even breathing in the smoke was making her dizzy.
Her hunger was now a mixture of headache, nausea, and

fatigue. The headache had come on suddenly, a strong, piercing pain; she didn't know what had caused it.

She kept straightening up and putting her hand to her mouth every time a convulsive yawn rose in her, yawns that were so strong they made her jaw pop. She watched tiredly as the doctor washed his hands in a porcelain sink, pinched out his cigarette, and placed the stub on the glass shelf.

"Fischer really is a rich man," he said, drying his hands as he turned around. "He could easily afford a little something for the breakfast of someone giving blood for his daughter."

"What's wrong with her?"

"That I can't tell you, I'm not allowed to. It's not good, I can say that much. Have you given blood before?"

"No."

"Then don't be frightened. It will hurt a little, I'll have to open your vein; grit your teeth," he said with a sigh. "Pocket the money and the voucher, even though"—he broke off—"don't worry, things look worse than they are."

"About the money," she asked, "will I get it right here?"

"No, you'll have to pick it up from this man Fischer, this fisher for money, because—" He fell silent suddenly as the gurney was rolled in.

What was brought in appeared to be nothing more than a very pale face: dark, pretty hair above a snow white forehead, and two bright, narrow eyes. Her body just fit into the curved depression of the supporting canvas, so that the white linen sheet seemed stretched flat across the frame.

"Over here," the doctor called out. He directed the nun to stand beside the operating table and called to Regina, "Come here, please."

She stood up. "Lie down here, and free your right arm completely."

She unbuttoned the sleeve of her blouse, pulled the thin material up to her shoulder and quickly rolled it there.

"Yes, that's it, good," the doctor said.

It felt good to lie down, her headache let up a bit, and when the sister placed a pillow under her head she felt almost comfortable.

"Thank you, Sister," she said.

She noticed that the doctor's face seemed troubled. It was twitching slightly in a strange and weary agitation, and the corners of his mouth trembled.

"Squeeze," he said to her, "like this." He opened and closed his hand, spreading his fingers wide, and she imitated him, as she watched him staring intently at her arm.

"That's good, that's good," he called out suddenly, "see how it's standing out, Sister, that's good, it'll be easy to enter. Now here . . ."

He stepped over to the young girl's stretcher and said softly, "Squeeze, squeeze, Fräulein Fischer . . . like this." Once more he demonstrated how it was to be done, and Regina peered intently at the solemn, almost hopeless faces of the nun and the doctor as they observed the thin, white arm rise limply, and the small hand clutch convulsively.

"Slowly," the doctor said, "much more slowly. Like this." He spread his strong, red hands out slowly and evenly again and watched the girl's arm. He sighed.

"Can't see a thing, that's no surprise. Let's get started anyway. There's no point in waiting. Let's go," he said.

"Turn your head to the left," he said to Regina. She did as he said, and stared at a green, thinly whitewashed wall to which brush hairs were still sticking—thin black lines, clearly visible, looking like some ugly pattern— and in the midst of all this hung a ceramic madonna, a crudely made, arm's-length piece of fired clay. The madonna held the child at a perpendicular angle so that its oversized ceramic halo covered her breast, leaving only her face visible. Regina was tired; she could tell that she was about to fall asleep, her eyes were almost closed. She fought hard to keep them open: the image of the Mother of God floated before her in the thin, ugly greenness, as if in water. . . .

She jerked to the right suddenly as she felt the needle enter her arm, and saw that the doctor had inserted the end of a rubber tube into her vein with a broad needle that was flat and beveled, almost like a quill. . . .

"Squeeze."

She squeezed and felt a rubber band being tied about her upper arm. She smelled the clean, impersonal odor of the nun, who must have been standing at her head.

"Hurry up with that, tie it tighter," the doctor called out, but blood was already spraying out thick and red onto the rough material of his white smock.

"Damn," he said, but the tourniquet was now tied fast around her arm and she realized that it wouldn't be possible to sleep. She kept her head turned to the right, heard him call out "Squeeze!" and saw him insert a needle in the thin white arm, pull it out again, call out "Squeeze!" again, several times, insert the needle again and again in the arm, then pull it out. His rough face was covered with beads of sweat, and it stood red and damp beside the white face of the nun, who was holding on to the tube and now attached it to a round glass housing shaped like an hourglass. . . .

She cried out softly as the tourniquet on her upper arm was suddenly released, and watched calmly and intently as the limp tube swelled, saw her blood pulsing into the glass container, a dark fluid that gathered and foamed, that seemed to flow away strongly and rapidly. . . .

"Tie it back up!" the doctor called out. "Tie it back up!" And she saw how the level in the little glass tube dropped and the other limp rubber tube leading to the arm of the girl filled with a steady, softly pulsing movement.

The procedure seemed infinitely slow, and she felt a deep and inexorable fatigue that disappeared each time her numb right arm was suddenly suffused with blood, blood that gathered in the glass tube above, welling forth from her. . . .

"Good," the doctor murmured a few times, "very good." And she saw in his face an expression that struck her as strange, one she hadn't expected: an expression of joy, true joy.

"Good," he said, "very good, if she can take it. . . ."

At times she tried to turn her head completely to the right to see the girl's face, but she saw only the nun's clean, dark blue smock, and cried out again softly as the tube with the needle was removed from her vein. . . .

"Good," she heard the doctor say again, "that's really good. . . ."

SHE FELT LIKE she was spinning in a circle, slowly at first, her feet the fixed point at the center of the circle her body was describing with increasing speed. It was something like the circus act where a powerful gladiator seized the lovely lady by her ankles and whirled her about.

At first she could still recognize the greenish wall with the red ceramic spot of the statue, and on the other side the green light at the window; white and green alternated before her eyes, but then the boundaries quickly blurred, the colors blended, and a bright green-white rotated around her, or she rotated around it, she couldn't be sure, until the colors were racing so fast they flowed together and she was spinning horizontally to the floor in an almost colorless flicker. At the same time she felt new pains in her ears, her body, her throat: it was as if the hunger, that mindless harassment in her stomach, had a magnetic power to release new pains. She felt tender all over, raw and exposed, and she realized with shock that she wasn't going to lose consciousness.

Only when the movement slowed down did she notice that she was lying where she had been. Just her head, her head alone, seemed to be spinning; she had the impression at times that it was lying to the side of her body, disconnected from her, at times at her feet, and at certain moments it lay where it was supposed to, on top of her neck. Her head seemed to be rolling around her body, but that couldn't be right either; she felt for her chin with her hands and touched it, the bony protuberance. Even when her head seemed to be lying at her feet, she could feel her chin. Perhaps it was only her eyes, she didn't know. The only certain thing was the pain, which gradually coalesced, without losing any of its essence, so that she could no longer separate it into throat, ear, body, or head pain. The nausea too was actually almost chemical in effect, a disgustingly sharp acidity that rose in her throat like a barometer and then receded again, only to rise slowly once more.

Nor did it do any good to close her eyes. When she closed her eyes, it wasn't just her head that reeled, she felt her chest and legs join in the crazy spinning. But when she kept her eyes open, the consciousness she never lost allowed her to recognize that the section of wall immediately in front of her eyes always remained the same: a portion of greenish, whitewashed wall with a chocolate-colored frame higher up that bore, in dark brown script upon the lighter background, a motto she couldn't decipher. The letters were squeezed together here and there like the microscopic print of an eye doctor's chart, at other times they swelled into disgusting dark green sausages, expanding quickly until it was impossible to grasp their form or sense; they grew so fat they burst beyond legibility, only to shrivel the next instant into tiny flyspecks that never quite disappeared. This portion of the wall always remained the same: the light green color, the chocolate frame and the script, alternating from thick to thin, and she realized that she couldn't turn her head either, even if it seemed she could. . . .

She gave a start as she realized that she was lying in exactly the same spot as before, without having moved an inch, and had been completely motionless: everything was calm, everything was in place again. She saw her chest, and the dirty brown leather of her shoes below, and her gaze fell directly on the script on the wall, which she could now read: *Your doctor will help you, if GOD helps him.*

"I T' L L B E A mess," she heard the doctor say. "She's going to vomit soon."

If only I could, she thought, but the sharp acid taste still only rose to a certain point in her throat and then retreated; it was choked back in a sort of spasm, a spasm over which she had no control.

The pain in her head was now piercing, very sharp and definite. It seemed to have concentrated in a spot above her left eyebrow, and the piercing pain kept jerking her back from her weariness; she wanted to sleep, to sleep. . . .

She couldn't see the doctor and she didn't dare try to move her head; the sweet fragrance of his cigarette still hung in the air, eating its way into her alert consciousness, as did the motto, dark on light green: *Your doctor will help you, if GOD helps him.* Then she closed her eyes and the word *God* remained in her. At first it seemed to be script, three large, dark green letters, standing in the darkness behind her closed lids, then she no longer saw the script, and it remained in her as a word, sank within her and seemed to sink deeper and deeper, yet it remained, it fell and fell, never reaching bottom, and suddenly it was with her again on top, not script, but word: *God.*

God alone seemed to have remained with her through all the types of pain she could no longer keep separate in her mind. She felt herself beginning to cry; the hot tears dropped quickly from her eyes, ran down her face, and from the way the tears fell, because she couldn't feel them on her chin or throat, she knew she must be lying on her side. Now her fatigue seemed to grow greater than her pain, which the tears appeared to relieve, and she knew that now she would fall asleep....

XII

FISCHER DREW ASIDE the curtain and set the madonna on a stack of thick books in the light, so that it was illuminated from all sides. He smiled. He still hadn't forgiven himself for not knowing of its existence till then. For years it had stood in a church only fifteen minutes from his lodgings, and he'd never discovered it. To be sure, it had been hidden in the sacristy, in the midst of thuribles, vulgar monstrances from the rococo period, and insipid plaster figures. This small fifteenth-century madonna was charming, its market value could scarcely be guessed at, and owning it was wonderful. He was happy; he smiled faintly, and for the first time it occurred to him that some true kernel of religious feeling must indeed animate the cult of the madonna among the common folk, this strange, meltingly sweet worship that had always repelled him, though he couldn't say why. . . .

The statue before him, standing in full light, with its intense red-and-gold decoration, was delightfully simple in feeling: the face was truly virginal, beautiful, and maternal. He'd never realized, never observed, that these three traits converged. Here it was obvious: virginal, beautiful, maternal—and with a shade of suffering that did not distort any of the three; suffering, and that trinity of traits he knew from theological treatises and the Laurentian litany, but had never seen portrayed.

At that moment—although he didn't tend toward emotional extravagance—the statue seemed to him the most beautiful of all his many art treasures, this carved and painted piece of linden wood scarcely as tall as an encyclopedia volume, that had now been extracted from the ruins of the sacristy, its magnificent deep red and golden colors slightly scratched. He walked slowly around the desk and examined it closely from every angle. It had no visible faults, nothing unnatural or exaggerated in its form, in the natural beauty of the figure, in the fall of robe, in the position of the arms, the curve of the throat, and the strange humble pride of the arch of the neck, the carriage of the head, that extraordinarily beautiful face expressing the paradoxical trinity, which seemed to him for the first time no paradox at all. Even the child in her arms pleased him, although in general he didn't like depictions of the baby Jesus. They were failures as a rule, overly sweet or overly clumsy—just as living children seemed to him overly sweet or overly clumsy, either kitschy or coarse.

He stepped nearer and examined the child in the Blessed Virgin's arms more closely. It was scarcely longer than his index finger. In spite of everything, he had to overcome a slight distaste. Secretly he objected to artists who placed babies in the arms of such small statues, even when they were correctly proportioned—they always reminded him of embryos.

He bit his lip, drew up his chair hastily, and sat down. He felt himself turn pale; this series of happy and joyful, almost religious, thoughts was abruptly interrupted, and he was overcome once more by the other feeling, a mixture of boredom and disgust. His gaze still rested on the little statue, but he no longer saw it. . . .

He gave a start as he heard a knock at the door. He snatched up the small figure from the table and set it on the top shelf of the bookcase behind a row of large tomes, where it was completely hidden. . . .

"Come in," he called out.

The moment he saw the proof sheets in the hand of his secretary, boredom surfaced again, an infinitely gentle despair mingled with an infinitely gentle bitterness.

"The proofs, Herr Doktor," said the young man, "for the first issue of *The Lamb of God*, they've just arrived."

The young man peered at him expectantly, a pale, delicate fellow who appeared both devout and intellectual, a combination he usually found appealing, but which repelled him today.

"Thank you," he said, taking the rough proofs. "That's fine."

He could tell from the odd bend of his back, and the set of his head, that the young man was hurt.

Well, after all, he thought as the secretary left, this first issue of *The Lamb of God* did represent an achievement. Paper shortages, difficulties securing permissions, a desperate search for authors and a capable printer in a city that seemed deserted—all this had been overcome in six weeks with the eager assistance of this young man—and in the midst of it all came the confused day of the surrender, bringing with it new and unexpected political difficulties. In spite of everything they had managed to publish the first issue of *The Lamb of God.*

He picked up the proof sheets and let them glide through his fingers one by one, bored. Well, his secretary would do all that, read the proofs, arrange the makeup into pages; he laid the sheets aside, retaining only the title page. It bore a vignette of the Lamb of God that had headed the title page for fifty years now, a frightful bit of kitsch; it could be found in every library and in the bookcases of Catholic families. They spilled out of portfolios, lay covered in dust on top of cupboards and in storerooms, a million copies displaying this vignette, which was a truly ghastly engraving: a closely shorn lamb with a weary expression and a devoutly lowered tail, against whose neck was propped a pennant bearing a cross.

"His Eminence the cardinal begs you to accept this little statue as a gift for having succeeded, in the face of so many difficulties, in getting *The Lamb of God*—ah—back on its feet," the canon had told him. "We're expecting great things from this first postwar journalistic venture. . . ."

HE LAID THE title page aside as well, and only now did it occur to him that he had been bequeathed a small treasure for managing to collect and print up a few feeble essays beneath that vignette. But the irony of the fact gave him no pleasure. He was tired; boredom and despair seemed to blend more intimately, a sluggish stream without end, whose bitterness was not sufficient to give it savor. . . .

The telephone rang. He picked up the receiver and answered.

"St. Vincent's Hospital," a voice said.

"Yes," he said, suddenly agitated. "What is it?"

"She's fine," the unknown voice said. "Your daughter's doing fine. She's much better. Dr. Weiner gave her a transfusion; it was a total success. We'll know by this evening whether her condition is permanently improved."

"Thank you, Sister," he cried, "thank you. I'll take the liberty of coming by this evening. Give my greetings to my daughter, please."

"Of course. You'd indicated there'd be a bonus for the blood donor, may I send her to you?"

"Certainly," he said, "certainly, I look forward to giving her that small token of my appreciation. Is there anything else?"

"No. Until this evening, then."

"Good-bye," he said, and hung up. . . .

The brief joy had already faded as he hung up the receiver and heard the soft metallic click of the cradle. The feeling returned, like deep water in which he was standing immersed to his neck, its tepid, endless surface rising to his mouth: boredom, nausea, and just a touch of sensual pleasure. . . .

IN WARTIME THERE had been moments in which life had been almost beautiful, or at any rate dangerous and at risk, at risk daily, a risk that was all the more attractive because it was attended by infallible safeguards: a strong air-raid shelter, money, provisions, and the certainty that he would always be on the correct side politically, no matter how things turned out. Of course he'd been in the Party, he'd even had a few conferences with the Nazis—they'd seemed nice enough fellows in their own way, for that matter—but at the same time he secretly possessed a long written statement from the archbishop saying he had joined the Party at his suggestion, almost at his insistence, on a religious mission, as it were. . . .

Since the war had ended, things were going so smoothly that it sickened him. It was so easy to earn money that he was overcome by contempt and nausea each time he took a bundle of banknotes from the safe, counted them out, and locked it up again. It would have been ludicrous to open a controlled bank account; an attic half filled with artworks, stuck up there because he didn't like them, brought in more money than he'd realized in the old days from the sale of two farms. . . .

The old days, he thought, lit a cigar, and flipped through the proofs of *The Lamb of God* again without seeing them. So many things had given him pleasure in the old days: reading Goethe, writing down his reactions to what he'd read, polishing those thoughts and seeing them in print, or building up a religious journal, watching it grow, even if he then had to lay the finished product in the laps of weary and incompetent church officials. These days nothing held any interest for him. . . .

He turned his cigar in his fingers and gave himself up to his memories, gazing at them as if they were photos of the boring life of a stranger. They produced an infinite tedium: an entire trunkful of pictures that meant nothing to him, although he was forced to look at them. An endless chain of infinitely long afternoons seemed to open out before him, filled with the tedium of an overstuffed stomach, and the sound of a piano played by a novice damned to fumble on in mediocrity for all eternity.

Only when he thought of his wife did a feeling of hatred rise in him, goading him, warming him for a few moments, but for a few moments only, for he felt pity for her as well, this beautiful woman with the profile of an Italian princess. . . .

Boredom, nausea, and a touch of sensual pleasure: boredom, disgust, and the faint titillation that a bundle of banknotes aroused in him, while he realized that boredom was always the predominant element in the mixture. It always took up the most space, while the other ingredients—sensual pleasure, disgust, nausea, pity—appeared minuscule, smothered by its leaden weight. . . .

For a moment he recalled the madonna, but at the same time the word *embryo* surfaced, chasing all the other words away, holding the field: ugly, awakening neither boredom nor disgust, but fear. It had always repelled him because of the *y*, which seemed to give the *o* some lewd meaning. It seemed like a secret word taken from some foreign language, inserted to express a whole complex of concepts as disgusting as they were mysterious, a shorthand code for the horror that would surface and pursue him whenever he thought of the madonna, of any madonna, or of that one. *Madonna* would always be paired with *embryo*, a beautiful word with an ugly one, producing each other like mirror images. . . .

It occurred to him that he needed to get the fifteen hundred marks, and he stood up. He unlocked the safe, let the heavy door swing open, and took the banknotes from the piles: ten fifties, twenty-five twenties, and fifty tens. . . .

He went back to the desk, placed the money in a drawer, and as he pushed it closed it struck him that, contrary to the old saying, money smelled, in fact it smelled strongly. He noticed the smell every time he opened the safe, a sweet, faint odor, sweet and soiled, impersonal yet rich in associations, faint yet surprisingly insistent. When he opened the door an intense, sweet cloud would emerge, mawkish filth, awakening in him the image of a brothel—but it occurred to him that it was the smell of blood, the extremely diluted and refined smell of blood. . . .

HE FELT A slight sense of relief when he thought of Elisabeth. Her name, her memory, released a strange tenderness in him he could neither understand nor explain, and yet it remained. A joy tinged with irony filled him, although he was furious at her for having discovered his deepest secret in the playful, effortless way she discovered everything. . . .

At any rate the fact that she stood current common practice on its head struck him as eccentric indeed: instead of investing money in objects of value, she converted objects of value into money and gave it away. She sold family belongings, took money from rental properties, withdrew from accounts, put pictures and furniture on the black market, and dedicated herself to a new humanistic sport: distributing bread coupons.

This hysterical behavior struck him as ridiculous, yet also impressive in its sovereign manner, bearing the traits of true eccentricity. She was stubborn, and he was secretly pleased by the war she had declared against him and the old man—

A cease-fire, she'd said.

It would be dangerous if she managed to scare up the soldier who'd brought Willy's testament. Willy's body could be dug up, his identity determined, and the moment his death was officially certified his will would be legal and valid, as long as it couldn't be proved that the military seal or the name of the officer had been falsified. . . .

HE TAPPED HIS fountain pen against the lampshade to summon his secretary, and when the pale, devoted fellow appeared in the door he said in a friendly tone, "I'm sorry, Windeck, I was thinking about something else. I'm very happy the first issue of *The Lamb of God* is coming out, you mustn't think I fail to appreciate your part in our mutual labor. Would you like a cigar?"

The secretary smiled happily, selected a cigar from the box held out to him, and said softly, "Thank you, Herr Doktor. . . ."

"Go ahead, take another one. . . ."

He took another one.

"By the way, a woman who donated blood for my

daughter will be here soon—give her this money in exchange for the hospital's voucher and get a receipt—fifteen hundred marks. . . ."

"Certainly," said the secretary.

He didn't see his boss lay down his cigar and prop his head in his hands. . . .

XIII

THE HIGH, GRAY flank of the church had crumbled between two supporting pillars, thick and tall, and bright gray daylight filled the opening as if it were a gigantic gate: chunks of stone lay at the base like blasted rock. There were heaps of rubble everywhere, but at the entrance he found they had been partially cleared away, and he walked across the smooth, white flagstones through piled-up debris toward the wooden door that led to the interior and pushed against it. He was caught by surprise. The door had been knocked off its hinges and was merely propped against the frame; it pivoted at his touch and fell toward him. He caught it with an effort and leaned it back in place. Inside, all was still. Birds were flying about: he could hear their cries. Somewhere their young were peeping, and his gaze fell at once upon a battered candelabrum still attached to the vault above. The chain swayed, creaked softly, and he saw two fat sparrows rocking on the metal rim. They flew away as he walked on. Only a small area around the door had been cleared, the debris swept back; as he went on he had to climb over broken masonry, and he looked up as he entered the nave. The light coming through the huge gap in the side of the church fell harshly upon the destruction. The saints overhead had all toppled down, their pedestals were either empty or a few blunt and ugly fragments still stuck to the wall above: two legs from the knees down, the lonely stump of an arm that had been affixed with great care to the vault. A broad crack in the wall appeared sharp and black, running like the silhouette of a staircase from top to bottom. High in the vault the sky stood like a sharply jagged chunk of gray, and he saw a second deep rent that extended clear to the huge wound in the flank, narrowing, filled with bright light, opening out again, and he could follow the thickness of the wall precisely as it widened in descent from the vault until, at its base, it was a broad as a door, heavy and gray.

His gaze remained below: the altar was buried in debris, the choir stalls had been toppled by the blast. He saw their broad brown backs inclined in what seemed sarcastic prayer. The lower rank of saints on the columns showed gaps as well: abraded torsos and flayed stone, hideous in its mutilation and painfully deformed, as if it once had been alive. He was struck by the demonic grotesqueness. A few faces grimaced like furious cripples because they lacked an ear or a chin, or because strange cracks deformed them; others were headless, and the stone stumps of their necks thrust up horribly from their bodies. Equally disturbing were those who lacked hands. They almost seemed to bleed, silently imploring, and a baroque plaster statue was oddly split, almost cracked like an egg: the pale plaster face of the saint was undamaged, the narrow, melancholy face of a Jesuit, but its chest and belly were ripped open. The plaster had trickled down—it lay in whitish flakes at the base of the figure—and from the dark hollow of the belly straw spilled forth, saturated with hardened plaster.

He climbed on, past the communion bench into the apse on the left. The frescoes were undamaged; daylight fell full upon them. The wonderfully pale and yet glowing colors of an ancient fresco depicted the Adoration of the Magi. Still lustrous even in its faded state, with portions that were only faintly colored lines, he found consolation in the painting's undamaged state. The side altar too was unscathed, it even appeared to have been cleaned—the altar table was clear, and a bouquet of flowers stood in front of the stone tabernacle—and as he looked around, peering into the side aisle, he saw the dark confessionals leaning slightly forward, awkwardly tilted boxes covered with dust and bits of mortar, and far away at the end of the row of columns he saw a light he hadn't noticed up till then. He walked toward it. A candle was burning in front of a picture of the Virgin Mary, and beside it hung the large, wooden crucifix that had previously been hanging in the vault by the candelabrum. . . .

He brushed bits of stone and dirt from a bench and

sat down. The last time he had been in a church the war was still on; it seemed an eternity ago, although hardly a month had passed. The candle flickered restlessly before the shrine, whose wooden surface had been slightly warped by humidity. The varnish was already flaking off here and there, and the face of the Virgin was streaked with whitish weals—only the flowers were fresh and beautiful, wonderful large carnations with fat buds standing in swollen capsules. . . .

He tried to pray, but as he did, he was startled: he heard singing, beneath him. It was coming out of the earth. His shudder quickly passed as he remembered the crypt that was no doubt still undamaged, and he listened to the singing. The voices sounded delicate, filtered, angelic, they seemed few in number. They were singing a capella, and as he recognized the text of the song, and the melody as well, he remembered that it was May, still May—the month the war had ended. . . .

He could tell from the voices that they enjoyed singing: a second verse followed the first, then a third, and he was sorry when it came to an abrupt end. He sat in silence and the stillness fell around him, oppressed him. He wished they had gone on singing.

He was afraid. The gaping cracks suddenly struck him as dangerous; he felt they might widen, the vault come crashing down and bury him with these mutilated statues. He broke out in a sweat. The vault actually seemed to tilt—he stood up, crossed himself hastily, and ran to the door, over the flagstones toward the heavy wrought-iron railing. . . .

From the other side of the chancel he heard the people emerging: they were laughing and talking together, and then he saw them: a tiny group of gray shapes that quickly dispersed, leaving only the black figure of the priest. . . .

He sat down on the stone base of the fence and waited. He knew that the rectory was situated behind him, and he had just seen that it was occupied. Although his hunger had faded, leaving only a gnawing, faintly dizzy sensation, he decided to ask the priest for something, bread or potatoes, or a cigarette. He saw the figure approaching; seen from below he looked tall, the black robe flapping about his legs, two shoes, large, with turned-up toes, pathetic and ugly. . . .

THE PRIEST WAS startled to see a figure suddenly rise before him, his thin yet swollen face grimaced nervously, and he clutched his hands around the thick hymnal. . . .

"I beg your pardon," said Hans. "Could you give me something to eat?"

His gaze wandered across the priest's sloping shoulders, past his large ears, to the square in front of the church: old trees in bloom, their trunks half buried in rubble. . . .

"Of course," he heard the priest say. The voice was hoarse and weak, and now he looked at him. He had a peasant's face, thin and strong, a thick nose, and remarkably beautiful eyes.

"Of course," he said again. "Will you wait here?"

"Yes." Hans sat down again. He was amazed. He'd made the request because it occurred to him that the priest would have to try to help him, but he was amazed to find that someone actually existed who would agree without hesitation to give him something to eat. . . .

He watched the figure cross the street, turn to wave to him again from the front steps. . . .

The prospect of food had awakened his hunger again: it rose in him, that strange, intense, yawning void that caused his cheeks to tighten in a spasm, that cloud made of air, that insistent belch that left a bad taste in his mouth and filled him with hopelessness at the same time. Eating is an inexorable necessity that will pursue me throughout my life, he thought; he would have to eat daily for the next thirty or forty years, at least once a day. He was burdened with the thousands of meals he must somehow provide, a hopeless chain of necessity that filled him with fear. He had already been roaming about the ruins of the city for nine hours that day without finding anything, not even what had been promised him. It was an appalling struggle that he would have to renew on thousands of occasions, and not for himself alone. For the first time he thought of Regina, and her image stood clearly before him, inescapably beautiful and compelling: her blonde hair and pale face, slightly distorted by mockery as he appeared in the dark opening of the door to ask, Would you like some bread—a cigarette? He longed for her, suddenly, intensely, painfully, and he imagined himself kissing her. . . .

The smile on the face of the chaplain seemed otherworldly, almost as unreal as the clear and pure singing that had risen to him from the crypt. He felt himself taken by the shoulder and pulled along; he was overcome by weakness and stumbled slightly as he followed the hurrying figure. They went around the curve of the sanctuary, a half circle that seemed infinitely long to him, and descended the stairs; he felt the coolness of the thick walls and gave a start as the chaplain placed his fingers, damp with holy water, upon his palm. . . .

"Are you Catholic?" asked the chaplain, crossing himself.

"Yes," he said. "I was baptized in this church."

"That can't be."

They paused in the entranceway.

"Yes, really."

"My God, then you must be. . . ."

"Yes," he said with a sigh, "this was my parish church, before I went to war." He thought fleetingly of those distant Sundays that he had spent at his mother's side in the semidarkness of this comforting Romanesque space. . . .

"And now?" asked the chaplain.

"Now I live outside the city in a suburb. . . ."

"Come this way."

He followed the chaplain into the dim, arched vaults where the pews stood crowded together: the daylight entered only faintly, and at the front the tiny reddish flame of the Eternal Light flickered in front of the tabernacle. The chaplain gestured for him to follow him into the sacristy and he simply nodded toward the altar, too tired to bend his knees. It was brighter inside, a light bulb was burning, and the smile on the chaplain's tired, peasant face seemed like a grimace of pain. . . .

"I'm pleased you're here," said the chaplain.

He pointed to a dark brown bench in front of a low wardrobe whose curtain was not closed. He saw bright robes for the children's choir and the white lace garments of the priest, all looking slightly dusty.

"Yes," the chaplain said eagerly, and his tired face was enlivened somewhat by his enthusiasm. "It's true: I'm pleased you're here."

He shoved open a door and pushed aside a few scrolls of dusty drawings. "No one's asked me for anything yet today, and I have two additional packages from this morning's offering here—let's see now."

His black sleeves now fluttered closely about Hans's face, laid a few packages wrapped in brown paper on the table, and the chaplain said, "Take whatever's there and remember: they're not from me, I'm not the one you have to thank. . . ."

"Who, then?"

"Thank God—unknown persons—ones whom we could well call the, um. . . ."—his face flushed a bit in embarrassment—"the living church"—his eyes narrowed with excitement—"sinners perhaps, perhaps saints—who knows, poor people—perhaps even rich ones. . . ."

Hans picked up the packages from the table and tried to untie one, but his fingers were without strength; he felt paralyzed by a sudden weakness.

"I can't do it," he said. "Can you do it for me?" The priest's broad hand pulled a string loose, carefully untied a knot, and revealed the contents: a small wrinkled apple, which rolled across the table, a thick slice of bread, very thick, almost as thick as the hymnal lying beside it, a cigarette wrapped in tissue paper, and a pair of military socks, washed and darned, the stripes encircling them a glowing white. . . .

"There," said the chaplain, "there."

Hans tried to pick up the bread up with his fingers, but he couldn't. It seemed infinitely thick; the crust, brown and rounded, surrounded it like the encircling wall of a fortress, and there was no point in trying to grasp it, his hands were too small. The cigarette lay on the smooth surface of the table like a gigantic, white, cardboard cylinder, a cigarette advertisement fallen from the side of some building, far too large. His hands lay on the table, small and dirty, far, far away from him, and the voice he heard was equally distant. The voice said, "Drink this."

He felt something flowing into him, mellow and cool and yet still releasing warmth, a wonderful drink, its taste somehow familiar, although he had forgotten its name. He felt his tongue touching his moistened lips, and drank again, and again it flowed into him, wonderfully mellow and cool, and suddenly he knew: it was wine . . . wine.

The objects on the table took on their true forms again, a slice of bread as thick as the hymnal, an apple, a cigarette, a pair of socks. His hands filled with strength and life, and he became aware of the chaplain's perplexed face, quite close to his: ashen and weary, reddish pouches under the eyes. He saw the glass, lifted it, and drank.

Wine, he thought, lowering the glass suddenly in fright and setting it on the table. He stared at the chaplain.

"Don't worry," the chaplain said with a smile. "Don't worry, it's wine—just wine—would you like some more?"

"If you think so."

"Why not? It's just wine."

He took a long sip and watched as the priest opened a second package: he unfolded a square kerchief and a banknote fell from it. His eyes were so clear again that he could see the "50" and the yellow stripes of the kerchief. . . .

"Do you have enough wine—I mean for the mass. . . ."

"Oh, yes," said the chaplain. "Don't worry—enough for years to come." He put the things back on the table. "All we need are a few drops, and we managed to save our whole supply—and there's even new wine. Are you married?" he asked with a smile, unfolding the kerchief fully and holding the bright, gauzy material before his face. . . .

Hans said nothing for a moment, then replied, "Yes."

There was a moment of slightly embarrassed silence as the chaplain refolded the cloth. Hans set the glass back on the table. He looked at the priest, and suddenly he felt an intense, burning desire to be with Regina.

"I have to go," he said. "Please excuse me. . . ."

Hans took the package from the table and said, "Well . . . I . . . we'll see one another again, I hope. . . ."

"I really hope so—I'd like to meet your wife. Wait a moment. . . ."

He went into one corner of the sacristy, carefully withdrew a key from his pocket, and opened a large, dusty cupboard. He returned with a reddish, gleaming bottle, held it out to Hans, and said, "You haven't had anything from me yet—please take this."

"Does it really belong to you?"

The chaplain laughed. "Not entirely, I rescued it, you might say, from the cellar of a burning house. The owner gave it to me later, I think it's mine to dispose of as I wish. Good-bye," he said. . . .

Hans paused for a moment at the door and watched

as the chaplain locked the sliding doors of the cupboard.

"Don't wait for me," he said. "I'm staying here...."

Hans left. He bowed slightly before the altar, and outside, as he tried to walk faster, the bottle, cold and heavy, kept bumping against his thigh.

XIV

ALL AT ONCE he heard her arrive. Her step was weary, she lingered for a while in the hall; she seemed to be removing her overcoat and hanging it on the coat hook in the dark. Then her footsteps approached his door and he felt his heart pounding, strongly and evenly. She paused before his door. He would have liked to have seen her face, and he waited, expecting her to enter and check on him, but the footsteps withdrew again, and he heard her go into the kitchen. . . .

He'd wanted to get up the moment she arrived, but

he couldn't. Joy seemed to paralyze him. He lay there and felt only the beating of his heart. . . .

Shortly afterwards she came into the hall and began chopping wood. He could picture everything precisely; the way she placed the crudely cut logs on the floor and struck at them blindly in the dark, not splitting the wood, just chopping off small splinters. Just so she doesn't hold on to it in the dark, he thought, and hit her fingers. The ax was dull, he knew that, but she could still cut off a finger or hurt herself badly. He heard her begin to curse softly. She missed several times, hitting the floor with the heavy ax, making the walls and floor tremble slightly. At last she seemed to have enough kindling; she tossed the ax in the corner and went back into the kitchen. . . .

Then everything fell silent, the darkness was almost total now, the shadows in the room were deep blue, like dark smoke. They settled in the corners of the room; he could no longer see anything but the area around his bed, everything dirty, the walls cracked, and now he noticed for the first time that the ceiling had an actual hole in it.

He stood up, walked quietly over to the door, and opened it cautiously. Light was coming from the kitchen. The old, blue coat that she had draped over the windowpane let large, yellow beams of light in through its tattered holes, and the rays fell onto the debris in the hall: the ax blade gleamed somewhere and he saw the dark logs, their split surfaces glowing yellowly. He approached slowly and now he could see her. He realized he'd never seen her like this before. She was lying on the couch with her legs drawn up, wrapped in a large, red blanket, reading. He saw her from behind. Her long, damply shining hair seemed darker, tinged with red; it fell across the arm of the couch. A lamp stood beside her, and the stove was lit. A pack of cigarettes lay on the table, together with a jar of marmalade, a loaf of bread that had been cut into, and beside it the knife with its loose, black handle. . . .

SUDDENLY HE KNEW that he would see her his whole life long. He felt a sort of dizziness; he could easily imagine her as an old woman, still slim, her hair gray, and the round, slightly mocking face. This realization moved him deeply and painfully, and he sensed something inexorable, as if someone were pouring cold water on a hidden part of his inner self, like a dentist rinsing a tooth he'd just been drilling on: it was both a pleasure and a shock. He felt as if he'd seen her this way many years ago, and would see her twenty years from now, time and again—he had risen from his bed, had done something irrevocable, something he could never undo. He had accepted life, it was concentrated for him here; a brief span of infinity, filled with pain and happiness. . . .

She was smoking a cigarette in a holder she apparently held in her mouth. From time to time she would roll over and dip her head in a hawklike movement to shake off the ash. He saw her clear yet soft profile, and all at once he wanted to kiss her again. But he didn't move. He knew well what entering the kitchen would mean: he would be forced to live, to take upon himself the infinite burden of days that couldn't be paid for with a few kisses, to tread the boards of daily life, the theater of the black market, of work or theft, while he had thought to sleep beneath the stage, in the shadows, below the footfalls of the players. . . .

He knew there was still time to disappear, to sneak quietly down the stairs and out into the night. Perhaps she wouldn't even be very sad about it, she surely wouldn't expect him to return again. . . .

He smiled without realizing it. It seemed to him that he was seeing her for the first time. He was still wearing her coat; he wore it because he had no other. It smelled of her. Silence reigned, she turned the pages slowly, then she laid the cigarette holder aside and now he saw that she must be holding a cup on her stomach. The fire in the stove had intensified—he could hear it hissing—and overhead the wind howled through the ruins. It swept down chunks of masonry and plaster from the broken roof and damaged areas of the building; they fell with a clatter among the rest of the debris.

She'd placed the cup on the chair and was reading again. She read very slowly. He grew impatient, and as he watched he recalled that he had once been a bookseller, and that he had had another wife, his colleague at work. He'd gone to the cinema with her a few times, or had taken her home when they'd had classes together—it was all infinitely long ago, in another life. He couldn't imagine that he had ever taken anything seriously: a course of study, a profession. He remembered his intense shyness and inhibition when he walked her home, the woman who later became his wife. On autumn evenings in the lighted city he had longed to caress her tenderly, but he hadn't even dared to offer her his arm. At times they passed along darker streets, and at a brightly lit station they boarded a tram, talking all the while of books, films, and lectures they'd heard. She wasn't pretty or elegant, she was small and ordinary, and the gentle light of the streetlamps fell among the trunks of the trees, yellow, dissipating, flowing, almost liquid, and between the light and the trees, those gray, soft trees, the fog stretched its long, lush tendrils like smoke, slowly spreading, almost smoldering, as if arising from a smothered fire. Then he'd walked home along the river, very slowly, sticking close to the granite balustrade that crowned the embankment, and nearby, invisible in the fog, the rushing water flowed on calmly, steadily, and he always threw his cigarette stub as far as possible out into the fog, where it expired with a hiss in the void. . . .

She still hadn't moved. Once she pulled the blanket a bit higher and tucked it in, and he registered this childlike, impatient movement as something new. . . .

He entered suddenly without knocking, went straight up to her, and kissed her on the mouth. He felt her soft, slightly moistened lips and saw that her eyes were open. They were dark gray, shimmering and somewhat slanted, and there was something doll-like about the way her glistening violet eyelids jerked upward. He kept his eyes on her as he kissed her firmly; he had grasped the back of her neck and felt her smooth hair between his fingers. He gazed at her for a long time, and she didn't look down. Only later, when she had let the book fall and he bent farther over her, only then did she close her eyes, and he was startled to see in her face the signs of tender rapture. . . .

He released her and felt himself blushing.

"Sit down," she said. She'd straightened up, pulled the blanket away from her legs, swung her feet around, and was now sitting up. He couldn't understand why he was so happy to see her. He took her cup from the chair, placed it behind him on the table, and sat down.

She said, "You're laughing, you're smiling, what's the matter?"

He said nothing. He felt the pleasant warmth of the stove behind him.

"My God," she said again, stood up, started to pick up the jar of marmalade, the bread, the knife, then left them all where they were, and he saw her hands up close for the first time: they were small and slender, very childlike, almost shockingly small. Her hands were trembling. . . .

"You're hungry, surely?"

"Yes," he said, straightening up and looking at her. Her eyes were moist.

He took a cigarette from the package she'd left on the table, tore a strip of brightly printed paper from the jar of marmalade, and twisted it into a spill. She looked at him. . . .

"How long were you away? It seemed so long, longer than the whole war. . . ."

He snuffed out the spill, laid what remained of the burned paper on the end of the table, and stood beside her at the stove. . . .

"I'll make coffee," she said.

He simply nodded. She seemed slightly embarrassed; suddenly they felt like strangers. She lowered her eyes, pulled up the zipper of her green sweater sharply, smoothed her rumpled skirt, and patted her hair. The water was bubbling. She put a spoonful of powder in the pot and began pouring the boiling water into the pot from a cup with a missing handle. . . .

As the coffee's fragrance reached his nostrils he realized he was almost ill with hunger. He sat down, knocked the ember from the end of his cigarette, and stuck the stub in his coat pocket. . . .

She poured in the rest of the water, placed the tin cap of the marmalade jar over the pot, and sat down beside him. She began to spread the marmalade on her bread, slowly and carefully, but he saw that her hands were trembling. She laid the bread on a small, yellow tile, peered into the coffeepot, and then poured for him. . . .

"Drink with me," he said gently.

"What?"

"Join me." She smiled as he passed her cup over to her and poured. . . .

At the first swallow he felt a strong attack of dizziness: the bit of bread and marmalade seemed to have fallen into some hidden recess of his body and thrown him off balance. He was very dizzy. Everything was spinning around even though he had his eyes closed; it was a powerful but not unpleasant rocking motion. He seemed to be swinging back and forth in some dark, gloomy space like the clapper of a bell.

He opened his eyes again, took a sip, took another bite of bread, and the more he ate and drank, the more the swinging and swaying ebbed. . . .

He took another piece of bread and marmalade and could tell he was feeling better. The coffee was wonderful. He pulled the cigarette stub from his upper pocket and said to her, "Could you give me a light, please?" She picked up the spill from the edge of the table. . . .

"What have you decided?" she asked. "What do you want to do?"

"I haven't thought it out yet, but I'll do something. I'm even glad."

"Really?"

"Really," he said, "I'm glad to be doing something; we'll talk about it. Here." He took the kerchief out of his pocket and unfolded it in front of her. "I want to give you this. . . ."

"How beautiful!" she said. She took the kerchief in her hands, spread her fingers, and let it lie across them like a veil. "Beautiful," she said, "very beautiful. I'm very happy. . . ."

"I have wine too," he said. "A whole bottle of wine, some bread, and an apple."

"An apple," she said, "that's really a rarity; there aren't even any apples on the black market right now. . . ."

He stubbed out his cigarette and stood up. "Come with me," he said softly. "Will you come with me?"

"Yes," she said. He stood waiting by the table and watched her take the candlestick from the cupboard, put the cigarettes in her pocket, and take the matches; her face was very serious, she was almost crying. He noticed, and went over to her. "If you don't want to," he said, "if you don't want to come with me—I won't be angry. I love you very much."

"No," she said, and he saw that her lips were trembling, "I really do want to go with you. . . . I'm just sad. . . ."

"Why?"

"I don't know," she said. He opened the door, turned off the floor lamp, and pushed her gently forward, holding her by the shoulder. In the dark hall he held her firmly until he'd opened the door to his room and turned on the light.

"Come in," he said.

He released her shoulder and gestured with his head. She approached slowly. He shut the door behind her. . . .

She sat down on the bed, and he moved the table closer to it so that she could rest her arms on it. "Do you have glasses?" he asked. . . .

"Yes, in the cupboard there." She pointed toward a corner still dark in spite of the light. "In a box—there's a corkscrew there as well."

He rummaged around in the dark in the dusty-smelling cupboard until he knocked against the box, which rattled.

"Bring them here," she said. She took the glasses from him and wiped them carefully with the kerchief. He saw them shining in the glow of the lamp as he opened the bottle. He filled the glasses and sat down beside her.

"Well," he said softly and raised his glass, "now you're my wife, is that what you want to be?"

"Yes," she said earnestly, "that's what I want to be."

"I'll never leave you as long as I live."

"I'll stay with you, I'm glad."

They smiled at one another and drank.

"A good wine," she said, "very smooth and fine."

"It's Communion wine," he said. "It was a gift."

"Communion wine?" she asked. He saw that she was startled; she pushed the wine away and looked at him.

"Don't be afraid," he said, laying his hand on her arm for a moment. "It's only wine. Do you believe in it?"

"Yes," she said. "I believe in it. Don't you?"

"Yes . . . I was afraid at first too, but not anymore."

"At times," she said quietly, "I've wished I didn't

believe, but I can't help it: I do. I just wish I could drink the wine if it were more than wine. It makes me very sad."

"Me too," he said. "I'm sad. We'll often be sad."

She drew the glass to herself and drank with him.

"Really," she said, "I'm afraid."

THEY LAY AWAKE for a long time, smoking, while the wind howled in the building, loosening fragments and causing bricks to tumble; sections of plaster came sailing down from the upper stories, crashing to the ground and shattering to pieces. He saw only a glimmer of her, a warm, reddish glow when the cigarettes flared briefly: the soft outline of her breasts beneath the blouse, and her calm profile. At the sight of the firmly closed, narrow groove of her lips, that small, black valley in her face, an infinite tenderness filled him. They tucked the covers snugly about them and nestled together, and it was wonderful to know that it was warm and that they would be warm all night. The shutters banged and the wind whistled through the holes in the windowpanes and howled through the broken rafters, and somewhere something clanked loudly and steadily against a wall, something metallic, and she whispered at his side, "That's the gutter, it's been broken for a long time." She was silent a moment more, took his hand, and went on softly, "The war hadn't started yet," she said. "I was already living here then, and when I came home I saw a section of the gutter hanging there and I was always thinking they'd have to have it repaired, but they hadn't fixed it yet when the war started. It just hung there at an angle, one of the clamps had come loose and it seemed it would fall any moment. I heard it every time the wind blew, every night there was a storm, and I lay here. And after every rain I could see the traces of the water clearly on the side of the building where it had flowed at an angle against the wall, a white path edged in dark gray that led downward past the window, with large, round holes to the left and right, their centers white, with increasingly darker rings about them. . . . Later I was far away, I had to work in Thüringen and in Berlin, and as the war was coming to an end, I came here again, and it was still hanging there: half the building had collapsed. I'd been far away, far, far away, and had seen a great deal of pain, death, and blood, I'd been afraid—and all that time that damaged gutter had been hanging there, guiding the rain into the void, because the wall no longer existed. The roof tiles had been blown off, trees had been uprooted, plaster had crumbled away, but this piece of tin had clung to its one remaining clamp for six years."

Her voice softened, almost singing. She squeezed his hand and he could tell that she was happy. . . .

"Many rains had rained down in those six years, many dead had died, cathedrals had been destroyed, but the gutter still hung there, and I heard it banging in the night when the wind blew. Can you believe I was glad?"

"Yes," he said. . . .

The wind had suddenly died down, all was still, and a chill crept quietly and imperceptibly nearer. They pulled the covers higher, stuck their hands beneath as well. Now nothing could be seen in the darkness, he couldn't even make out her profile, although she lay so close beside him he could feel her breath: the warm exhalations reached him calmly and steadily. He thought

The Silent Angel   *139*

she'd fallen asleep when suddenly he ceased to feel her
breath and groped helplessly for her hand. And he felt
her move her hand from up around her head or chest,
grasp his, and hold it firmly. With a happiness he'd never
known before he felt its warmth, and knew he would
never be cold sleeping beside her. He nestled closer to
her, pressing up against her so tightly that she had to
lift her hands, since there was no longer room for them
between their bodies. He could no longer feel her
breath and thought she must have turned her nose upward, and be staring toward the ceiling in the dark, and
for the first time he asked himself, What can she be
thinking? He hoped that she was happy; he loved her,
and he knew that she loved him, but he knew nothing
of her thoughts, and he would never know them, not
even a portion of the innumerable thoughts that formed
in her mind during the long hours of the days and
nights. He felt very alone, and he had the impression
that she was not as alone. . . .

And suddenly he realized she was crying. There was
no sound; he could only tell from the movement of the
bed that she was wiping her face with her free left hand,
but even that wasn't clear, and yet he knew that she was
crying. He sat up, and immediately felt the cold air
blowing in under the door toward the bed; he bent down
close over her, felt her breath again, spreading against
his face and flowing gently past it like a stream, so that
he felt its soft touch back to his ears. Even when his
nose brushed her ice-cold cheek he still could see nothing; the darkness about them was now total, and suddenly he had one of her tears on his lips. He had always
heard that tears were salty, salty like sweat, and sometimes sweat had run down his face into his mouth, and

now he knew that tears were salty, salty and warm like sweat.

"Lie down," she said softly. "You'll catch cold, there's such a draft...."

He stayed over her. He wanted to see her, but he saw nothing until she suddenly opened her eyes: then he saw the soft gleam of her eyes and the shimmering tears. He lay back down slowly and then sat up as he again sought her hand, which had slipped from his. She lay without a sound, and he knew that she was still crying; from time to time she brought her left hand quietly to her face. He turned to her quickly and blew in her face and thought he could sense her smiling. He blew again.

"That's nice," she said, "nice and warm." She blew in his face as well, strongly, and it really was warm, and felt good. For a long time they blew back and forth into each other's faces....

Then he kissed her in the dark, but he felt a slight, barely perceptible resistance and slipped back into his former position.

"I think I really do love you...," he said.

"Oh yes," she said. "Really, I love you...."

Suddenly he had to yawn. It rose in him like a spasm, an infinite weariness. She laughed and put her arms around his neck, and he felt that she was yawning too. He brushed her cheek with a kiss, and it seemed to him as if he'd never kissed her before, she seemed like a totally unknown woman....

He put his arm around her shoulder, pulled her close to him, and fell asleep, his face pressed against hers, and in their sleep, they exchanged warm breaths like caresses....

The Silent Angel 141

XV

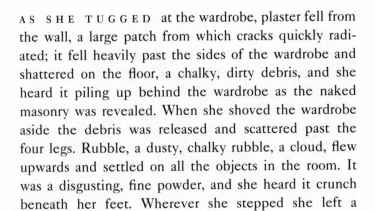

AS SHE TUGGED at the wardrobe, plaster fell from the wall, a large patch from which cracks quickly radiated; it fell heavily past the sides of the wardrobe and shattered on the floor, a chalky, dirty debris, and she heard it piling up behind the wardrobe as the naked masonry was revealed. When she shoved the wardrobe aside the debris was released and scattered past the four legs. Rubble, a dusty, chalky rubble, a cloud, flew upwards and settled on all the objects in the room. It was a disgusting, fine powder, and she heard it crunch beneath her feet. Wherever she stepped she left a chalky pulp that lodged itself in the broad grooves in the floor. . . .

She felt the tears coming to her eyes; an unknown, painful, undigested lump of despair filled her throat, a clump of pain that wanted out, but she swallowed hard and went back to work with a grimace. She opened the window, swept up the plaster, driving a white cloud before her, and began wiping everything a second time with a dustrag. She was secretly cursing the sudden impulse that had led her to clean the room. Where had it come from? She didn't know. This desire for order and cleanliness was totally new, and she knew that it was senseless. Everything had seemed cleaner before: spots and ugly circles were now visible where she had damp-mopped the floor, ancient, ground-in chalk that hadn't been noticeable before. All her efforts had served only to reveal a strange, transparent film of repulsive stains that appeared ineradicable. The furniture too seemed shabbier than before now that she had wiped it clean a second time; chips and splintered areas came into clear view for the first time. It was all ugly junk, hardly worth cleaning: the damaged bed, the table with its loose top, which had to be moved carefully or the legs would come unglued, and both wardrobes, tall, brown boxes, spotted with chalk, warped by the rain, and littered on top with bits of plaster that were constantly falling from the damaged ceiling. . . .

An infinite expanse of dirt appeared that now threw her into despair, and against which all struggle was useless. The wallpaper was tattered and the plaster filled with cracks; in some sections it was held in place only by the glue that was supposed to bind the wallpaper to the plaster, but now held the plaster itself.

As she shoved the second wardrobe cautiously aside, she heard only a faint trickle; bits of plaster that had gathered behind it rattled to the floor, a few handfuls of rubble. . . .

She hauled bucket after bucket into the room, but she only needed to mop up a few square feet and the clear water had already turned milky and thick from the loose chalk, plaster, and sand, and each time she poured out a bucket on the rubble downstairs a stubborn sediment remained that was hard to rinse out. Each time she brought fresh water into the room she stopped in shock: the places she'd mopped had dried in the meantime and shone with a white, ugly roughness, while the floor she had yet to clean was dark and even in tone.

There was a steady trickle as well from the baseboards, a particularly fine debris, a small amount of which proved sufficient to turn an entire bucket of water white and ruin it for further cleaning. . . .

Something akin to obstinacy made her carry on the struggle, keep carrying bucket after bucket, although she knew inside that it was senseless: the spots always returned, and new bits kept falling. She only realized how much chalk and plaster, cement and sand was involved when she had cleaned up a new area and carried down a full bucket of dry debris that had fallen behind the bed, leaving only a small, naked patch on the wall. She could tell by touch that the plaster lay loose beside the wall: there was a cool, dark gap between the plaster and the masonry that she could insert her hand into, and when she tapped on it, it gave off a hollow, mysterious sound. The ceiling was uneven; it had sunk in places beneath the weight of the plaster, forming cracks and gaps, an entire geography of finely branching lines that would one day break and fall, generating new quantities of dust, new masses of chalk to be awakened by water on the floor, a white, ineradicable stain that would break out again and again like a persistent rash. . . .

Later on she lay on the bed smoking, her face turned toward the wall so that she wouldn't see how senseless the long hours of her torment had been, this torment that would go on and on, forever. The clock on the dresser showed five o'clock. She had worked for seven hours, carried countless buckets of water, driven by this urge that struck her as new and terrible, and the floor showed all gradations of tone from gleaming white to the darkest gray in a diabolical irregularity, a stained and spotted monument to her efforts.

Her clothes clung to her body; they seemed pasted on like thin rubber, giving her no room to breathe, and she could smell herself: the sour smell of sweat and dirty char-water. An intense desire for good soap and clean clothes brought tears to her eyes. She pinched out her cigarette and slowly ate some bread, plucking one crumb after the other from the thick slice and shoving them into her mouth. . . .

It was raining outside. Darkness invaded the room and softened the irritating traces of her senseless cleaning, and when she had eaten the bread, she lit her cigarette again and lay back on the bed, smoking and dreaming in the murmur of the rain. She couldn't stop the tears from coursing down her cheeks; they flowed in streams, incessant, hot, then quickly cooling. . . .

She gave a start as she awoke, sat up, and saw that it was six o'clock. It seemed to her that the water stains on the floor had grown darker, and although it didn't look clean, a certain smooth regularity seemed to reign. She longed so for cleanliness; it was that desire that had driven her to start in the first place, but it seemed senseless, it kept welling up, without ceasing. The dirt would not retreat before the cleansing, but seemed instead to consider it a challenge, doubling itself, tripling. As the sun suddenly broke through outside she was startled to see that the wardrobes were cloudy, as if covered with grease, and the floor revealed the full splendor of its diabolical patterning. . . .

She stood up wearily, put water on the stove, threw on some wood, and reviewed her treasures as the water heated: half a bottle of wine, half a loaf of bread, some marmalade, a lump of margarine, an entire cup of instant coffee that she had carefully tied up in wax paper, tobacco and cigarette paper, and money; money, in the drawer, a small pile of dirty bills: almost twelve hundred marks and the fifty that Hans had given her. Her riches seemed to her substantial and comforting. . . .

She held the soap to her nose for a long time, rubbed it dry against her face and cheeks to sense its fragrance close up, the fragrance of this thin, fissured slice, permeated with the essence of almond. . . .

She heard him set something heavy on the floor outside, a sack apparently, which seemed to contain something hard and heavy, and as he entered, she saw that it was raining outside again—his face was wet, and black coal dust had mixed with the rain, black rivulets ran down his pale and weary face; it seemed as if he were weeping black tears. She saw this through the thin soap lather clinging to her brows and lashes, making her blink, and she was embarrassed by her bare breasts and with damp hands pulled up the nightshirt that had slipped down. Smiling, he kissed her on the neck, and for a moment they saw themselves in the mirror side by side, his dark head on her shoulder next to her pale face. . . .

THEY ATE IN bed. Next to the coffeepot on the chair stood the small stack of bread slices spread with reddish marmalade. The air was sweet and mild. It was raining outside, and the sound of the steady rain was like a magic spell. The dark circles on the ceiling were visible again, as always when it rained, silently expanding circles, absorbing, growing until the puddles that stood in the ruined story above were emptied. The silent, quick way the water appeared, as on a blotter, was somehow disquieting; the circles seemed like eyes staring at them, dark at the center, at their core, almost black, with a dangling droplet that finally fell, shading toward an increasingly lighter gray at the edges. They seemed like signals, signs of warning that flared up, remained for a few days, and disappeared again, leaving only their dark rims; then later a patch would occasionally loosen, plaster would fall to the floor, sending up a spray, leaving behind the bare lath-work, a dark gap that gradually filled with cobwebs, and where the plaster had already fallen down, water dripped straight through. They had moved the bed—now it stood in the middle of the room—and this increased the impression of floating uncertainty. . . .

They lay side by side without touching. Just being clean filled them with happiness; he only touched her face or arm from time to time, when he handed her bread, and she smiled at him.

"By the way," he said, "your discharge papers passed close inspection."

"They did?"

"I got a registration certificate in exchange for them, even though"—he laughed—"even though I'm apparently the first person to have been discharged. They didn't expect anyone until the middle of June. I think we'd better alter the date now, and wait till June, but I got the coupons."

"Good," she said. "How long are they good for?"

"Until the end of June—who knows what things will be like by then. . . ."

"Yes," she said. "That's almost a whole month—by then—and the coal?"

He laughed again. "It's easy. All you have to do is jump on the trains and throw the briquettes down, sometimes the trains even stop, and they're hardly ever guarded. I watched everything carefully, all afternoon long. Someone even told me the exact time the trains arrive"—he reached into the pocket of the coat hanging over the back of the chair and took out a piece of paper—"Five in the morning, then around eleven, just past four in the afternoon, and around six, they're generally on time. You need a cart. You can't go at five because of the curfew. Do you want some coffee?"

"Yes," she said.

She took the cup from the chair that stood on her side of the bed and held it out to him. He poured.

"Yes," he said, "who knows what will have happened by the end of June, by the middle of June even. We have money and coupons, bread and tobacco, and I'll gather a hundred briquettes of coal a day, that ought to be enough. I've heard you can get a loaf of bread for fifty briquettes, and a cigarette for ten."

"Yes," she said. "I think that's right. Bread costs thirty marks, and a cigarette six, and coal is cheap in the summer. . . ."

"It goes up in price when the temperature drops—but then bread goes up as well—hunger's worse in the winter."

"Let's not think about winter yet."

"No," he said. "For God's sake let's not think about winter."

"I'm very happy," she said slowly.

"Me too," he said. "I don't think I've ever been as happy."

They fell silent a while, and the sound of the rain was as strong as ever, dripping trees stood in the damp twilight outside, and there was a splatting sound each time a drop released itself from the ceiling. . . .

"Do you want a smoke?" he asked, but she didn't answer, and when he turned around he saw that she had fallen asleep. She was smiling in her sleep, and he moved nearer, until her warm face lay on his chest. I love her, he thought, I know her, and I'll learn a lot more about her, but no matter how much I know, it will never be much, almost nothing.

XVI

HE WAS VERY tired. It had been a long time since
he'd been up this early. He was practically asleep. It
was very cold, and even the rigid, almost imperceptibly
flickering flames of the slim candles seemed frozen.
They stood yellow and steep, thin and sickly before the
bluish darkness behind the altar; there seemed to be a
whitewashed wall or a faded curtain there, he couldn't
be sure. The candlesticks were worn as well, as crude
as the somewhat slanted tabernacle they flanked. The
people crouched or knelt there silently, and some of
them smelled bad, the way hungry people, living in

stuffy rooms, smell: like cabbage and cold smoke from the stove. The necks he saw before him were thin, hair curled from beneath the kerchiefs of the women, and in the humble, musty stillness he heard the voice of the priest speaking calmly and evenly, as if time were of no importance: *Corpus Domini nostri Jesu Christi custodiat animam tuam in vitam aeternam. Amen.*

He had never before heard a priest say the entire sentence before each communicant. Most of the time they just murmured, mumbling as they moved along, but this one paused in front of each person receiving the host and spoke the entire line. The Communion seemed to take forever. The doors behind him weren't airtight, either; there was a draft. Cracks in the walls and the windows had been boarded over and the plywood boards had been warped by moisture; they had swollen, loosening in varying layers, and a filthy pulp oozed out between the layers: the glue that had originally held them together. . . .

Toward the front, where the altar was, a Gothic arch leading to the central nave must have been bricked up or covered over with a large curtain; he still couldn't tell whether it was a wall or only some sort of cloth façade. All that could be seen were the gilded sides of an imitation Gothic column thrusting upwards in a pointed arch, its end points meeting directly over the altar.

Everything was happening so slowly. The priest was still passing out the host to the few people who had come to the Communion bench, and his voice still murmured solemnly and at length over these poor gray heads, while he held high the thin wafer of the host: *Corpus Domini nostri Jesu Christi . . .*

The acolyte had turned up the collar of his surplice

and appeared to be rubbing his wrists under the broad folds of his sleeves to keep them warm. He could be heard sniffing loudly at regular intervals as well. The priest intoned the final lines of prayer with raised hands, and the responses of the acolyte came forth sullenly and indifferently. He lifted his head slightly from time to time and seemed to cast a sidelong glance at the candles, as if he disapproved of this waste of wax. Finally he knelt in front with the missal on his arm and the priest made the sign of the cross over him, slowly and solemnly. . . .

In spite of everything, Hans experienced something akin to peace and joy. He saw the boy hastily blow out the candles and then follow the chaplain into the sacristy. Outside the day was bright, it must have already been nearly eight. He crossed the street and rang again; inside, behind the iron grate of the door, he heard the sound of the bell, hollow and shrill. The housekeeper, a woman with a broad, red face, opened the flap, looked at him inquisitively, and asked, "Is mass over?"

When he said yes she pulled the door open without another word and called back to him as she turned and walked into the hallway, "Come in."

He followed her, but when he bumped against a wooden wall in the dark at the end of the hall she had disappeared, and he thought, I'm probably supposed to wait. . . .

From around some corner he couldn't see came the rattle of dishes, and suddenly he recognized the repulsive, dirty, sweet smell hanging in the hall, which had eaten its way into the half-tattered and apparently damp carpet: it was the smell of overcooked sugar beets. Steam billowed from around the corner where the kitchen must be, buffeting him with its noxious warmth. Apparently she was cooking beet purée the way almost everyone did—on a stove, stoked with damp wood, that didn't draw—for smoke and a rusty odor met him as well. And the deep voice of the housekeeper sang around the corner beyond which he was apparently not worthy to pass: *Rorate Coeli desuper.* And she answered herself with an even deeper basslike drone: *Et nubes pluant justum.* Her knowledge of the text evidently did not extend beyond these two phrases, because she kept chewing broadly at them again and again, droning them out. During the long pauses that she introduced—apparently to do something or other at the stove—he felt tempted to insert the Latin prayers that now came back to him from long ago. It must have been almost ten years back that the religion teacher had drummed them into his head. *Ne irascaris Domine . . . ne . . . ultra me,* those long-winded, half-spoken songs that unfolded more brightly toward the end, like tender buds, and against the background of his memories of those interminable prayers the housekeeper's voice resounded again as if on cue: *Rorate Coeli desuper. . . .*

Finally light fell into the hall from the outer door, and he recognized the tall, narrow shadow of the chaplain in the whitish rays. At the same time he saw that he was standing before a wooden partition behind which a crate of potatoes and all sorts of dirty rubbish appeared to be stored. The figure came closer, and as he felt his breath in the dark, and saw the pale face, he said, "It's Schnitzler."

"Ah, Schnitzler," said the chaplain quickly, with apparent nervousness. "It's good you're here. I'm glad. . . ."

The chaplain opened a door from which dim light emerged, and urged him in; he found himself facing a mad confusion of bed, chairs, bookcases, and a huge table that was covered with books, newspapers, and a sack full of carrots. . . .

"Please forgive the mess," the chaplain said nervously, "there's so little space."

He looked around slowly. The room looked truly awful—still, the bed was made, probably the only tidying up that paid off in this den. The floor was clean as well, insofar as there was a floor: perhaps thirty square feet of wooden boards with wide grooves in which the moistened dirt gleamed blackly, a sign that it had been dampened with char-water. Several of the books were placed backwards in the bookcase. He went over to turn them around. At that moment the chaplain came in with the housekeeper. He was carrying a tray with a coffeepot, two cups, slices of bread on a plate, and a bowl of runny beet purée. The housekeeper had an armful of wood and was holding a clump of wood shavings in her other hand. . . .

"You'll have a cup of coffee with me, won't you?" the chaplain asked. "It's cold, isn't it, cold for June." He laughed.

He was in fact hungry, and here in the room he felt the cold again. He said, "Yes, thanks." The housekeeper stuffed the shavings in the black mouth of a stove directly behind the bed, dropped a few small pieces of wood on top of them, and crumpled up a newspaper. . . .

"That's all right, Katie," the chaplain said. "I'll do that." She went out, and when she had closed the door, she could be heard singing again outside, obviously enjoying herself: *Rora*—then she must have disappeared around the corner.

The chaplain held a match to the crumpled paper, and the flame ate its way upwards through it, dark blue and hesitant; smoke came from below, and tiny, light gray clouds emerged through the lid on top.

"Please forgive me for making you wait," the chaplain said, "but the vicar is ill and I had to say the second mass as well; I didn't know that yesterday. I hope I haven't kept you from something important. . . . "

He was now standing in front of the stove rubbing his hands, and looked at Hans with curiosity. Then he lowered his eyes again and murmured, "You wouldn't believe how cold it gets in the church. I feel like I'll never get warm again. What's it going to be like when winter comes?" He was indeed pale, and his coarse mouth drooped wearily. Beneath the beautiful, sad eyes—the only beautiful thing about him—lay dark, reddish shadows. His lids were inflamed. The wood could be heard crackling in the stove; the chaplain reached under the bed, took two briquettes from a crate, and tossed them cautiously on the fire. He seemed annoyed that Hans wasn't saying anything.

"Are you sure I'm not keeping you?" he asked nervously.

Hans shook his head. "No," he said, "you asked me to come by sometime, I . . . "

"Of course," said the chaplain. . . . "I asked your— your wife, to let you know—just a moment." He stepped up to the table, filled the cups, and sat down. "Please have some bread and purée. . . . "

"I've already had breakfast—the coffee helps. It's hot."

"But do go ahead and eat something."

"No thanks."

Now the chaplain, using his left index finger and the knife like a pair of tongs, took a slice of bread and let the watery purée, which still looked warm, drip onto it from a spoon. He began to eat with great relish—from time to time he turned around, looked at the stove, and noted with satisfaction that the thin metal was beginning to glow. . . .

He ate slowly, like someone who wants to delay for as long as possible the terrible moment when he will no longer have anything to eat, and who knows that he will still be hungry. Moreover the beet purée seemed to make his teeth hurt. Now and then he would grimace, try to keep a straight face, and a pained grin would result. He washed down the final slice dry with hot coffee.

"But surely you smoke," he said as he dabbed up the last crumbs from the table with his broad thumb.

"Yes," said Hans.

"Would you bring that pouch here, please?" The pouch lay between a suitcase and a cardboard box that seemed to contain dirty clothes, on the bookshelf. It was filled with rough-cut, blackish brown tobacco. Hans brought it to him and pulled out his case. It held only a few small shreds of tobacco and a small, flat, yellow booklet of cigarette papers.

"You roll your own?"

"Yes," said Hans. The chaplain held the pouch out to him and started filling a pipe, then leaned back, cleared his throat, and said, "I don't know exactly how to begin, you'll have to excuse me. We don't normally ask the faithful to come to us, I think it's usually frowned upon—our superiors are sensitive about giving the least impression of proselytizing"—he cleared his throat more emphatically and wiped tiny white flecks of foam from his lips—"but I took the liberty because I know your wife and learned during my visit that it was you who recently came to me in the crypt. . . . We had to move out of there, as you see—the great gable of the upper church collapsed, and cracks appeared in the roof of the crypt—"

"I've seen it," said Hans.

"This church is very ugly." He shrugged his shoulders; evidently he preferred talking about something other than what he had in mind. "It's what remains of a hospital chapel—You didn't realize I knew your wife?"

"No . . ."

"I buried your child. . . ."

"It wasn't my child. . . ."

"Oh." He cleared his throat and fumbled about nervously with his pipe, which didn't seem to be drawing properly. "I buried it. Your wife is very religious."

"Oh?"

"Didn't you know?" He took the pipe from his mouth and looked at Hans in honest surprise.

"No," said Hans. "I didn't know she was particularly religious. We only spoke once about religious matters, quite briefly. . . ."

"And you aren't married . . . by the church?"

"No—nor by the state."

The chaplain said, "Hm," and put the pipe back in his mouth; the tobacco wasn't burning well, and drawing hard on it several times robbed him of breath for a moment. It took a while before the tobacco was finally glowing and actual clouds of smoke arose.

"You see," he said, "I'd already spoken with your

wife a few times, even before you came here. She's truly religious, even pious—you really didn't know?"

Hans shook his head in silence. The tobacco was strong, apparently home-grown and quick-dried; he felt a faint dizziness, and weariness rose in him like a poison, slowly spreading, stopping up all the openings of his consciousness. He took a sip of coffee, saw the chaplain lift his arm to pour again, and involuntarily stared deep into the loosely hanging black sleeve, saw a muscular, hairy arm and the shirt-sleeve rolled up to the elbow and thought, Why doesn't he roll his sleeves down if he's cold? The hot drink revived him somewhat, and now he realized that the chaplain had continued speaking, a few sentences that he hadn't heard, for at that moment he was saying, "The sacraments, I don't understand how a person can believe and not take the sacraments. Can you explain it?" But he obviously wasn't expecting an answer. "You surely believe too, don't you?" The chaplain gave him a sharp look and repeated the question more loudly and sharply, "Surely you believe?" Apparently he expected an answer to this question.

"Yes," said Hans, without thinking. In fact it hadn't occurred to him till just then that deep down he'd never ceased believing. All these things were self-evident to him, even if his weariness was often so great that they seemed of little consequence.

"Well." The chaplain smiled. "After all, that's no small matter." He smiled more broadly, the radiance of an inaccessible simplicity spread over his face once more, and he put the pipe down once and for all. "And you have an intercessor, one so effective you would no doubt be saved in spite of yourself."

Hans stared at him in confusion. He shook his head and stammered slowly, "My mother, of course...."

"Not just your mother—your father perhaps ... and others you don't even know about, but one you have for sure, without question. I tell you, you can pray to the little one—it's clear, theologically established beyond any doubt, that they are with God, do you see?"

Hans shook his head.

The chaplain stared at him, at a loss. Narrowing his eyes in consternation, he said, "The child—don't you see?"

Oh, thought Hans, he's talking about the baby. There were days when he didn't think about it at all, while at other times it was with him like a terrible pain, an ineffable sorrow for which he knew no name. He looked at the chaplain and said, "Yes, of course—but it wasn't my child...."

"Even so—you're living with the child's mother in the most intimate of human bonds."

It seemed clear to him that the child was in heaven. He didn't doubt that, a six-week-old baby would surely go straight to heaven. There was no need to talk that over—but it seemed silly to him that this little being was supposed to be his intercessor.

He placed the cigarette stub carefully in his tobacco case and asked, "Was that why you asked me to come?"

The chaplain nodded. "You must forgive me ... at any rate—I feel I have a responsibility."

Hans stood up with a sigh and stood beside the stove. "Are you short of coal?" he asked calmly.

"Oh, yes," said the chaplain, turning around so that they could see one another. "It's so expensive...."

"I'll bring you some...."

"Oh, you mean . . ."

"You won't have to pay for it, it doesn't cost me anything. . . ."

"You have professional access."

Hans laughed. He laughed loudly; it seemed as if he were laughing freely and heartily for the first time in a long time. He laughed so hard that he choked and fell into a fit of coughing. But the instant he saw the silly, smiling look of the chaplain again, he was overcome anew by laughter. . . .

"You must forgive me," he said, "but 'professional access' is a good one."

"Why is that?" The chaplain actually seemed somewhat offended. "It's always possible."

"Of course," said Hans, and he felt a sudden sorrow overcome him. He longed to be beside Regina, lying next to her, hearing her voice. "Yes," he said. "I have professional access to it, I steal it, that's how I make my living. . . ."

"I see," said the chaplain with a brief laugh. "I suppose that must be quite a strain?"

"It's not so bad, it's fairly easy. You just mustn't go overboard—if you have thirty pieces in your bag, no one pays any attention, but I get thirty three times a day, it's a very punctual, well-regulated life, I have my outfit like a railroad man, my bag and a lantern—and a timetable. I assume my post with the regularity of a civil servant. Evidently my modesty awakens respect among the police. I'll bring you briquettes. . . ."

"I'll gladly pay for them. . . ."

"No, no, I'd like it very much if you would—" He broke off and looked at the chaplain uncertainly. For the first time he felt something akin to affection, not apparently directed personally toward this man. They looked at each other and Hans felt his face go slack. The weariness consumed the last traces of tension in his skin, and he felt as if he were inside a loose, leathery hull that bore no relationship to him. He said softly, "I'd like to confess. . . ."

The chaplain stood up so quickly and vigorously that Hans gave a start. "Hurry, hurry," he cried out, "sit over here." His face showed joy and fear, and something like mistrust. He moved with haste and eagerness, as if he had to run to a stove and rescue a pan that was boiling over.

"Sit right here," he cried. He grabbed his surplice from the nail, shoved the coffee cups aside, and propped himself on his elbows. The way in which he hid his profile in the palms of his hands had something businesslike about it, something both rehearsed and unconscious. He whispered, "In the name of the Father, and the Son, and the Holy Spirit."

Hans repeated the words hesitantly and said, "Amen.

"I don't know when I last confessed."

"Try to remember. . . ."

"What year is this?"

"Nineteen forty-five," said the priest, without showing any surprise. . . .

"Well I know for sure that I confessed in 'forty-three, in winter, just before a battle. . . ."

"A year or two ago, then."

"Yes." He hesitated. His gaze kept sliding away from the hand of the priest, which was somewhat dirty from the coal, and his eyes locked firmly on the bread plate, hopelessly bare, the empty cups with the black dregs, and the gray tablecloth.

"For the most part," he said, "I've been bored. I neither prayed to strange gods nor betrayed my wife while she lived...."

"You had a wife?"

"Yes ... bored," he said, "bored beyond words ... no sacraments—no masses—the last mass was a year ago. Yes—one year ago. I've sinned against the Sixth Commandment a few times—I've stolen, stolen often during the war—and now the briquettes—I'm living with Regina now—but she's my wife," he added, somewhat more firmly.

Now he stared through his fingers, slightly spread because they were tired from being clasped so tightly, and he saw that the chaplain was smiling, although he couldn't know that he was watching.

"And your prayers?" asked the priest.

"I don't know...."

"Try to remember."

"I haven't prayed for a long time ... the last time was in sick bay, that must have been two years ago ... and the briquettes...."

"Hm," said the priest. "How many do you take? More than you need?"

"Yes, I trade them for bread and cigarettes...."

"And give some away?"

"Yes."

"Fine.... You mustn't make money with them ... a man has to live, you understand?"

"Yes." He fell silent.

"Is that all?" the chaplain asked softly.

"Yes."

The priest cleared his throat. "Boredom," he said, "doesn't come from God. Always remember that. It may well have some good purpose, just as evil may, even must, serve a good purpose in some mysterious way, you see. But boredom certainly doesn't come directly from God. Think about that. Pray when you're bored, and if at first you feel even more bored, keep praying anyway. Do you hear? At some point it will work. Just keep on praying—and get married. Take the sacraments, they're our sustenance here. And remember that you're not without your own merits. It's a form of pride as well, to think oneself so great a sinner as to be beyond mercy. A very special form of pride, one that's easily confused with humility. Don't you want to get married? Your wife is suffering as things are, believe me...."

"Marry us."

The chaplain fell silent. "I'm bound by law. We're not permitted to perform any marriage that's not officially sanctioned. Why not go through a civil ceremony...."

"My papers aren't valid.... They may ask for documents.... Marry us as we are...."

The priest sighed, and remained silent for a long time. "I'll do it," he said. "I'll do it in spite of all the laws— I can marry you on condition that you promise to have a civil ceremony later, and that you'll repeat the religious ceremony as well...."

"I promise."

"Good," he said. "Come to me with your wife—after mass—into the sacristy. Bring someone along as witnesses. Say an act of contrition...."

While the chaplain raised his propped hands from the

table and folded them, praying briefly and fervently, for hardly more than a moment, Hans tried to recall prayers of repentance he had once known, but without realizing it, he was murmuring to himself, "I'm tired, I'm tired, I'm hungry, I'm sick—have pity." But he was already speaking before he knew it, he must have had one of those brief attacks of fatigued dizziness, for the pale face of the chaplain, who had risen, already hovered over him, murmuring softly, "Jesus Christ be praised . . ."

He stood up immediately and faced the stove. It suddenly occurred to him that he hadn't received any penances.

"You didn't give me any penances," he said without turning around.

"Say one Our Father and one Hail Mary each day with your wife." His voice sounded impersonal, somewhat irritated and bored, and Hans found that comforting. He reached under the bed, threw two more briquettes into the stove, and said, "I'll bring you some—tomorrow morning, you must accept them from me. . . ."

When he turned around, he saw that the chaplain had taken his tobacco case and stuffed it full. He pressed in the large, slablike pieces of tobacco and snapped the lid shut. "Then you must accept this from me—my brother sends it to me; he grows it himself."

"Thanks," said Hans. As he said good-bye, he avoided looking the chaplain in the eye.

XVII

THE CANDLE FLAME was mirrored on the lid of
the small, golden box, a dull, warm light that was reflected on the wall, where it formed a dancing pattern,
a trembling ring that tried to escape but found itself
trapped, dancing wildly within a tiny circle. The nun
had sunk into herself, a dark monument of multiple
folds of cloth in which only the pale, broad hand seemed
alive, tapping her chest piously, emerging three times
from the flowing sleeve, disappearing once and for all
after the third.

The priest snapped open the lid like a pocket watch.

The flecks of light on the wall were extinguished, and the flat host made the eyes of the dying woman light up with happiness. She tried to lift her hands and tap her chest, but the pain paralyzed her; it cramped her body, her innards contracted as if squeezed by a fist that constricted in hate and seemed to consist only of pain, savage, crushing pain, which then disappeared suddenly and completely again, so quickly she was shocked and was seized by a strong attack of dizziness. It rose in a rapid rush, sprayed over the edge of the nightstand, flowed strongly to the base of the crucifix, staining one candle, but the greater part of the surge splashed over the side of the bed to the floor, forming a large, quickly spreading puddle in which the shiny nun's shoe stood like an island. It was blood, dark, black blood. . . .

The nun cried out, the priest snapped the box closed, and for a moment the ring of light danced again in its tiny prison on the wall, until the priest shoved the box under his robe. . . .

The sick woman herself had scarcely changed her position, nor did she appear to be soiled, except for a drop of blood that ran down her chin, black and sticky. She saw the box disappear and realized that she was shut off from this final consolation. For a moment that seemed to last forever she felt weak and without pain, until the invisible fist clutched her innards again, that fist that grasped something without substance: pain, a lethal void that could nevertheless burst and rise up under the savage pressure, shooting up quickly. Blood this time flowed heavily and stickily down her breast and was absorbed like ink by the bedclothes, a great, dark circle. . . .

The face of the priest seemed to stand alone. His

black robe melted into the darkness, and within this darkness stood his tired and shocked face. His hands were folded stiffly and correctly at the point where his chest must have been. . . .

"Bless me again," she whispered. . . .

He looked at the floor and saw the eager hands of the nun plying the cleaning rag: the damp, gray wad was not absorbing the blood. It seemed doughy, clotting quickly, rolling aside like some strange substance. . . .

He stepped nearer, blessed her, and whispered, "Don't be afraid, you've received the sacrament of penance, and extreme unction: give your pain to the Lord, who knows all human suffering. . . ."

"Yes, yes," she whispered. "Call the doctor." But just then she saw him enter. Beside his broad form came another, buttoning his white smock rapidly as he went. From the earnest yet weary expression on his face, and the free and easy gestures, she realized immediately that he was a specialist. She tried to resist as he pulled up her nightshirt and felt her stomach. His face, empty of all hope, was close to hers, lay almost on her breast, the conceited face of an old man with a well-rehearsed rite of the great doctor, a script he now followed: doubt, the raised eyebrows, pensiveness, weariness, as he tested the area around her navel with fingers spread. She cried out as he suddenly pressed in sharply. She felt his five fingers like five iron knives thrusting into her, she saw a hint of satisfaction in his face, and she whispered to him, "Go away . . . get away from me!"

But now he listened to her heart, and the blood rushed from her mouth across his back, no longer spreading, a solid clump that seemed already black and coagulated as it left her mouth. That didn't bother him:

he remained bent over her like a general studying a map even as the shells are already falling near his quarters, knowing that his retreat is still covered, that his medals are assured—and that it is the little things that swell a reputation. Self-control. . . .

Although he had long since determined all he needed to know, he remained bent over her for a moment, then raised up, drew the blanket calmly over her, and motioned his colleague to one corner of the room. . . .

"Do you have the X ray?"

"Yes, it's just arrived." He took the plate from the envelope, gestured for the nun to come closer with the candle, and saw that the priest was approaching the bed again. The candle flame gave a savage, reddish transparency to the opaque photographic plate, illuminating a strange, dark gray circle in which a series of solid, black points were visible. . . .

"Amazing," the specialist said. "It's amazing she's still alive. . . ."

"Here's the exposure that was taken four weeks ago. . . ."

The doctor motioned for the nurse to bend over a bit because her shadow was falling across the second plate, and tapped three times with his index finger on the reddish gray, blurred surface. "One, two, three," he said, "that's all, I took the X ray myself. . . ."

"And the second one . . ."

"Yes," he said. "It must have spread like—like warts that suddenly cover an entire hand, the ulcers—in my opinion—must contain a substance that creates new ulcers when it's exuded—like—like warts—perhaps of a nervous origin?"

The specialist didn't reply. He took the second exposure from the hand of his colleague, held both plates side by side, and murmured, "It's hard to believe that these two exposures were taken so soon after one another, if it weren't for the fact that . . . "

"I can vouch for it."

"Of course. And I'm familiar with the phenomenon—it's seldom observed, The destruction of the organ progresses with geometrical speed; it would be interesting"—he lowered his voice—"to have an X ray of her present state. At any rate to analyze the expelled blood." He grinned faintly. "I'm carrying a sufficient sample of it on my smock, after all. We have to speak with her father-in-law. Come with me, please"—he lowered his voice even further—"If only we could do an autopsy. Come along. . . . "

SHE SAW THE priest up close, but didn't hear him any longer; only his face was clearly in focus. Agitation and weariness seemed to be waging a tug-of-war, his lips were moving jerkily, but she understood nothing, and this rapid, silent stammering seemed to her like a lover's enraptured whisper. In the large, beautiful eyes of the chaplain stood fear and a simple-minded joy. . . .

"Money," she said. "I have a great deal of money. I'm giving it to you—do you hear me?"

She saw him nod, and the silent entreaty ceased. Now his lips merely trembled a bit. . . .

"A lot of money for you . . . not a penny for them—everything for you—give it away . . . all my money, do you hear?"

He nodded again. . . .

Then it seemed to her that Willy was standing beside

her, his sergeant stars gleaming in the darkness. He knelt, and she saw his silvery braid close up, two shiny bands shaped like horseshoes, with stars on green cloth. His face was pale and fallen, so disintegrated by weariness that she could no longer find a trace of mockery in it.

As he lowered his head, she saw the bare spot on the back of his skull, the scarred neck, and heard him say, "I love you as one loves a shrine—not you yourself— just a shrine, because I loved you once. I still know that." For a moment he raised his head again, then she only saw his neck. "It's just that I don't hate you, and that means a lot—I don't hate you and I wanted to say good-bye to you—to see you once more—we won't see one another again."

She wanted to lay her hands on his head, but she couldn't. Suddenly it was the face of the priest, framed by the sergeant's shoulder braids, and she heard another voice saying, "Don't think about money in the hour of your . . ."

"Yes," she whispered. "I'm thinking about money, I want you to . . ."

Willy's head stood there again, and the two heads now alternated like pictures being rapidly switched, and the voices alternated as well, one speaking intimately to her, the other more formally.

"Just so the old man doesn't get a penny, promise me that."

"When you appear before the throne of God to be judged, you mustn't—"

"I hate him—you've got to promise me . . ."

Along with Willy's voice she heard artillery fire falling

somewhere in the city, sharp explosions distinctly different from the sound of bombs falling. . . .

"Now I'll say the Apostlic—"

At the same moment that the voice returned, the artillery fire faded. . . .

"I have to go—well, then. . . ."

" . . . conceived by the Holy Spirit, born of the Virgin Mary . . ."

She saw the gray figure go to the door, open and close it, and as the door fell shut, the dull drone of the guns outside died away as well. . . .

"Descended into hell . . ."

The pain was a soft piercing that swelled like a siren's howl, that seemed to stir her intestines, grasping them, forcing them upwards. She felt it like a lump in her throat—she didn't know she was screaming, no longer heard his voice, and the last thing she saw were those silently moving lips. . . .

The hot, dark stream struck the chin of the priest in its upward arc; the disgusting and greasy smell of the blood assailed his nose, dizzied him, and he quickly rose, but it was too late. The buttons of his cassock were still open, and the wave washed against the front of his shirt and flowed heavily downward; he felt it thick and wet. He stood up, pulled out the golden box, and regarded it anxiously. It was stained. He grasped it carefully in one hand so that he wouldn't drop it and rubbed the soiled side on his sleeve, nervously and quickly, as he watched the nun bend over the bed so rapidly that the candles flickered and the slender silhouette of the standing crucifix grew larger. For an instant the shadow of the tiny crossbeam rocked high above, broad and dark on the ceiling, then the flame shrank again, the large shadow of the cross sank down along with it, shrinking too, and he saw another shadow: the candlesnuffer. It appeared like a large cowl, sank slowly downward, sinking over one of the candles, and the corner stayed dark, and the shadow of the crucifix shifted a bit to the left toward the bed, where only one candle still burned—

"Is she dead?" he asked softly. . . .

The sister nodded. . . .

"God have mercy on her poor soul. . . ."

He turned around. The man he'd seen briefly in the hall, a thin, black figure with an imperious face, approached slowly, and he was shocked to see tears in that old, stony face.

The father perhaps, he thought, and he stepped aside and let the figure through, and the nun made room as well. He could see the dead woman for the first time. The small face was yellow, the mouth still open, as if new surges of blood were still to come, and this open mouth, twisted in pain, gave the face an expression of infinite fatigue and disgust.

The nun made a sign to him to go, and he put the golden box back inside his robe, buttoning his cassock carefully as he left. . . .

XVIII

FISCHER LOOKED OVER at the door, and when
he saw that it was closed, he bent down and unlocked
the nightstand; he pulled out slippers, a pair of dirty,
rolled-up hose, and now, with his face close to the
ground, he saw that the traces of blood had not been
entirely cleaned up yet. A thin, dark crust still clung to
the floor. He sighed, looked up at the candle, and now,
as he shoved aside the chamber pot and leaned back
against the side of the bed, panting heavily, he felt
something like shame. He remembered all the stories
he'd heard about inheritance cases. He broke out in a

sweat; the slip of paper wasn't in the chamber pot, either. He gave a start as the lock clicked at the door, and while he was still down on the floor he discovered a suitcase in the half darkness beneath the bed. He lay flat on the floor, tried to reach the handle, but the suitcase was pushed clear to the back. It was no use, he had to, he had to lower his head, shove it under the bed, and feel his way forward with his hands.

Nausea swept over him, and now he lay prone in the dirt, in this repulsive, thick layer of dust, and as he crouched lower to creep forward a bit farther his nose touched the dust. Tufts of the carpet got in his mouth, and a fit of coughing kept him from finally seizing the handle of the suitcase. He held his breath, choked back his cough, grabbed the leather handle; for a moment all was still, and in the stillness he heard the door open and then close again. He remained lying there, heard a single step, then everything was quiet once more, and he considered the fact that someone was now standing there regarding his legs, his shoes, the ludicrous lower half of a male body lying beneath the bed. He cursed silently to himself, and the violent, ugly, inner stammering brought him relief. He thought words that he had never spoken aloud, whose existence he had only dimly recognized: "Shit, crap. . . ." It was like a release. He decided to crawl back out. He shoved himself backwards with one hand, holding the handle of the suitcase in the other, and let out his breath with a rush—a cloud of dust whirled up around him, dirt got in his nose and mouth. He had to sneeze. His collar snagged on a piece of mattress wire and he paused again, stammering senseless, disgusting profanities to himself, feeling, with a mixture of repugnance and pleasure, his sweat mingle with the dirt. He gave a jerk, felt his collar tear, and gradually worked his way out, keeping his back to the figure. He threw the suitcase onto the bed. . . .

"What do you want," he murmured over his shoulder while he wiped off his face and knocked the dust from his clothes.

He could hardly see anything. His heart was pounding, and only slowly did the agitated, rotating field of his vision fall back into place: the crucifix on the nightstand, the reddish wall. . . .

He continued to curse inwardly without realizing it, and without knowing why. He felt a sudden, intense pressure to which he yielded with a sense of relief, filled with a strange, sharp, almost virulent joy, the pleasure of forming disgusting words, reciting in singsong loathsome phrases from an unknown world that opened to him effortlessly, thinking them into himself; it was as if they were a ransom for his shame. He didn't care about anything else—just that scrap. . . .

He sat down calmly on the bed, wiping his face clean as his agitated vision cleared and the fixed image of a pale young man gradually came into focus, holding a soldier's cap in his hand and regarding him with hostility. . . .

"What do you want, then?" he barked out. . . . "Are you looking for someone?" At the same time he snapped open the suitcase, felt about inside the pockets in the lid, and looked at the young man inquisitively. . . .

"Frau Gompertz . . . I'm looking for Frau Gompertz, room sixteen—I was told. . . ."

Fischer's curiosity was aroused as he discovered a few books among the woman's clothes.

"Frau Gompertz is dead . . . ," he tossed back calmly.

Suddenly he remembered again how valuable that scrap of paper could be to her father and her siblings, how immensely important—his heart beat more strongly, the excitement was hot and suffocating in his throat. He felt like he wasn't going to find anything in this suitcase, and he rummaged around desperately among the underclothes, fished out a prayer book, and flipped through it rapidly. He didn't look up until the young man's shadow fell over him—then he stopped and scrutinized the pale face.

"Frau Gompertz is dead, what do you want?" he cried out, as the young man stepped nearer.

"You're looking in the wrong place," said Hans. Slowly he walked over to the nightstand, lifted the crucifix, and pulled the narrow, white slip of paper from beneath the base. "She kept it in the same place at home," he said.

Fischer felt his nerves begin to fail; he had to press his lips tight to keep from grinding his teeth, but behind his closed mouth he could feel his jaw clicking savagely. He saw the stranger stick the paper in his pocket, and opened his mouth with an effort. "You realize...," he stammered, "you want... you know what that document is."

"I know, Professor, I brought it to her myself...."

"You? Tell me, you... don't we know one another?"

"We know each other," Hans said with a smile, and turned to the door.

"Stop!" cried Fischer. Hans paused.

Fischer closed his mouth tight to choke back the involuntary spasm that made him grind his teeth, hissing his new-found curses inwardly, chewing with pleasure the phrases that rose within him like a literature of despair—and all at once he leaped at the man. He registered the total surprise on the man's shocked face and used the first split second to force him against the wall, to twist his arm while reaching resolutely into the stranger's left pocket with his free hand. He laughed aloud as he felt the slip of paper in his hand and ran behind the bed. He waited there, ready for battle, his fists raised like a boxer's, but the figure against the wall didn't move.

"It's worth nothing to you—do you want money?" cried Fischer. "Anyway," he added softly, "I don't believe it's genuine."

He received no answer; the man, whose name he didn't know, whose face he thought he'd once seen fleetingly, slowly drew away from the wall and walked to the door. . . .

HANS HESITATED AS he reached the large entrance hall, which was filled with light: to the left stood the smiling angel that had greeted him in the night back then. Hans paused. The figure seemed to be gesturing to him, or smiling at him from the side, and he turned to it slowly, but the fixed eyes stared past him, and the gilded lily didn't stir; only the smile seemed meant for him, and he smiled back faintly. Only now, when the figure was standing in full light, did he see that the angel's smile was one of pain.

He didn't turn around until he heard Regina's voice, and he was startled to see the joy in her eyes.

"Well," she asked, "what is it?"

"She's dead," he said.

"Dead?"

He nodded.

"It doesn't matter," she said. "We'll find someone else to be a witness."

He took her arm and went down the steps with her.

XIX

THE TALL, MARBLE angel was silent, although
the vicar gazed at him and seemed to be speaking down
toward him. He had hidden his profile in the black
mud, and the flat spot on the back of his head where
he had pulled himself free from the column gave the
impression that he had been struck down, and was now
pressing against the earth to weep or drink. His face lay
in a muddy puddle of water, his stiff locks were spat-
tered with dirt, and his round cheek bore a fleck of mud.
His bluish ear alone was spotless, and a piece of his

shattered sword lay beside him: a longish piece of marble that he had cast aside.

He seemed to be listening, and no one could tell if his face expressed scorn or pain. He was silent. A puddle slowly formed on his back, and the soles of his feet gleamed damply and bluely. At times, when the vicar shifted his weight and stepped a bit nearer to him, it seemed as if the angel wished to kiss his feet. But he didn't lift his face from the mud; he lay there like a soldier protected by a trench. . . .

"Let us remember," the vicar intoned, "that it is for us to mourn, not her." He gestured with his thick, white hands toward the grave where, between two Ionic marble columns, the coffin stood, covered with a black cloth, rain dripping from its tassels. "Let us remember," said the vicar, "that death is the beginning of life. . . ."

The acolyte behind him clutched the dark bone handle of his umbrella tightly, trying to twist and turn it with the movements of the vicar, but at times the rhetorical flourishes came so suddenly that he couldn't follow them, and the instant a drop hit the vicar's head, he would cast a reproachful glance behind him, where the pale youth held the umbrella like a baldachin. . . .

"Let us remember," the vicar cried toward the marble angel, "that we too, we too stand perpetually on the threshold of death. *Media in vita*, says an old medieval verse. Let us think back on her, the dear departed—beloved, blessed with earthly goods, living as part of a large and strong Catholic family, to which our city owes so much—let us think back on her, how suddenly she was called to God, who sent his invisible messenger to her—"

He fell silent for a moment, perplexed: it seemed to

him that the spotless, bluish marble cheek had moved in a smile, and the vicar raised his nervous gaze and sought in the collection of umbrellas the spot where the silk appeared to be smoothest and most expensive. . . .

"How surprised the family was by the sudden news of her death"—his eyes wandered past the umbrellas to the spot where a small group held up their unprotected heads to the rain—"how the poor must mourn to have lost their faithful and enlightened helper; let us not forget to pray for her, all of us, yes all of us, who may at any moment be surprised by that invisible messenger God sends to us. Amen.

"Amen," he cried again into the marble ear of the angel.

"Amen," said the crowd, and a dark murmur came as an echo from inside the little temple.

"Let's stand over here," said Fischer. "It's dry here." He helped his father-in-law and gave him the flat place on the bottom of the angel, while he himself stood on its back. They took their hats off as the vicar began the ceremony inside.

The marble angel slowly sank; his round cheek was pressed into the soft ground, and his spotless ear was gradually swallowed by mud. . . .

"I have it," said Fischer, "here."

Gompertz took the little slip of paper and read it over. His sad face twitched, and he murmured softly, "The final greeting from my son, a document of his hate, a hate I've never understood."

"Do you think it's genuine, then?"

"I've never doubted it." He slowly tore the slip to bits and shoved the pieces carefully into the opening of his glove. . . .

Inside, the sexton responded to the Latin prayers of the vicar, and they saw that the vicar was confused for a moment about where to throw the shovelful of dirt. Finally he cast it against the coffin, and the clods of dirt scattered over the marble flagstones. . . .

The angel remained silent; he allowed himself to be pressed downward by the weight of both men. His luxurious locks were enveloped by gurgling mud, and the stumps of his arms seemed to strain more and more deeply into the earth.

ABOUT THE AUTHOR

Heinrich Böll was the first German to win the Nobel Prize for literature since Thomas Mann in 1929. Born in Cologne in 1917, Böll was raised in a liberal Catholic, pacifist family. Drafted into the Wehrmacht, he served on the Russian and French fronts and was wounded four times before he found himself in an American prisoner-of-war camp.

After the war, Böll enrolled in the University of Cologne, but dropped out to write about his shattering experiences as a soldier. A master storyteller, he wrote a host of novels and short stories. He was President of the International P.E.N. and an eloquent defender of the intellectual freedom of writers throughout the world.

Heinrich Böll died in Cologne on July 16, 1985.

ABOUT THE TRANSLATOR

Breon Mitchell received the D. Phil. in Modern Languages from Oxford University and is currently Director of the Wells Scholars Program at Indiana University. He has received a number of national awards, including the American Translators Association German Literary Prize in 1987 and the 1992 ALTA Translation Prize.